Robert MacMillan

Unsuccessful Competitors

And other stories

Robert MacMillan

Unsuccessful Competitors
And other stories

ISBN/EAN: 9783744750950

Printed in Europe, USA, Canada, Australia, Japan

Cover: Foto ©Andreas Hilbeck / pixelio.de

More available books at **www.hansebooks.com**

Unsuccessful Competitors

AND OTHER STORIES.

BY "GOSSIP."

REPRINTED FROM THE "SYDNEY STOCK & STATION JOURNAL."

WM. BROOKS & CO., PRINTERS AND PUBLISHERS,

22 BRIDGE STREET, SYDNEY, AND

EAGLE STREET, BRISBANE.

1897.

GOSSIP.

✦ PREFACE ✦

THESE stories have been selected from the pages of the SYDNEY STOCK AND STATION JOURNAL by the votes of our friendly readers. They have each taught something or borne some comfort to the voters, so, trusting to this selection, we send out this little volume to a larger audience, that may, perchance, not be so kindly in its judgment. But, whatever the verdict may be, the volume will be welcomed by many in the bush, and for their sakes the writer is content.

CONTENTS.

Unsuccessful Competitors.

IT was at the social gathering, after a country show, that the chairman said, "Mr. Wildwind will now propose the toast of the unsuccessful competitors." Then Mr. Wildwind arose and made a speech about the men who had lost the day, in the crude, common-place of his class. Yet he felt in his soul that there was something true and high and holy to be said on the subject, only he couldn't say it. His hearers realised that, too, and at every opportunity they cheered for the "unsuccessful competitors," but in spite of that, it was a tame affair. These men who make speeches at country shows trust too often to "inspiration." But that is a delusion and a snare. If a man is going to speak well, he must speak wisely, and must do his level best by careful preparation. He must ask himself how his speech would look in print, by the cold light of day, when the glamor of the hour has vanished and the applause of his friends has been forgotten. You can't make a good, wise speech on inspiration. Every good thing on God's earth has to be bought—some with money, some with sorrow, and some with weary years. Gordon says—

> "For what's worth having must aye be bought,
> For sport's like life, and life's like sport :
> 'It ain't all skittles and beer.'"

No, my word it ain't!
The "unsuccessful competitors" in life are the ones who command my deepest admiration. The men who win are the ones to laugh, and it's easy to be pleasant when you've won ; but the man who fails is often the hero. The men who have failed have been life's victors ; the men who fail are the men

whose names make the sweetest music on the tongues
of their fellows ; the men who fail are the men who
make the world's success ! If you think that the
winners in life's race are the men who deserve the
greatest credit, then it shows that you haven't
looked beneath the surface at all. But there's a
sterling honesty in the hearts of human beings that
stirs me when I think of it. When a man does a
smart thing and succeeds, there's a multitude to do
him honour ; but the great heart of the mass is
untouched ; they sneer at him, they mistrust him.
Deep down in our hearts we love the unsuccessful
ones, the honest ones, the sterling ones. It's good to
be a success, but it's better to be true and have a
heart at peace. Do you remember that old poem ?—

> " They say that the world, this great big world,
>   Will never a moment stop
> To see which dog may be in the right,
>   But will shout for the dog that's on top "

Well, that's not true ! Our world, the pastoral
world of Australia, prefers the dog that's in the
right.

If you sit down to judge by every-day appearances,
the greatest failure of history was Jesus Christ ! He
lived a brief life on earth, preaching a pure and holy
doctrine that is far above us now, let alone above the
miserable sinners who put on airs in Palestine two
thousand years ago. See how his life ended. Some
of his followers thought he was the promised Messiah,
some hailed him as " King of the Jews," but see how
it all ended ! The life of the Nazarene went out on
the Cross in the awful darkness of Calvary, while he
cried - " My, God, my God, why hast thou forsaken
me ?" What a death ! Yet what name on earth is
more potent to conjure with to-day ? Christ was,
according to human standards, one of the most
" unsuccessful competitors " that ever ran in the race
of life, but who dares say that now, a couple of
thousand years later ? Bah ! pharisaism may triumph
for the hour, and the winner may crow, but the

" unsuccessful competitors" may turn out to be the best men after all. You can never tell till the numbers go up, and old Dame Nature is in no hurry to hoist the numbers.

Then look at that sturdy little tentmaker of Tarsus, whose name was Paul. He was a pig-headed, masterful man, who, from my point of view, held lots of erroneous opinions But his heart was true. He said : "God hath made of one blood all nations of men, for to dwell together on all the face of the earth." He was the man, probably, to whom we owe that XIIIth chapter of Corinthians about charity. He was a big man, judged by the standards of to-day, but look at him from his own time he was an "unsuccessful competitor." He was a man who worked for his tucker while he preached, and that kind of man commands my respect. He got beaten and starved ; was shipwrecked and despised, and ended up his career in a Roman prison, He was such a poor man, such a despised man, that nobody noted the manner of his death, but he stands head and shoulders over the world's great men to-day. In his life he was an "unsuccessful competitor," in his death he was a failure, but look over the pages of history and you will see that he was no failure. He was a strong, true man, and the ages have done him justice.

Look at Socrates in his cell, drinking the deadly hemlock draught that gave him freedom from a world of envy, malice and uncharitableness. Socrates was an "unsuccessful competitor," judged by the light that shone in his prison house on the day of his death ; but what says the world to-day? The Socratic methods were wise ones. The man who drank the hemlock at the command of his foes was a hero, whose name will live forever. The men whose names are most revered on earth to-day are the men who were "unsuccessful competitors " in the race of life. Sir William Wallace, the idol of every Scottish boy, failed in his life's work, and was executed on

Tower Hill, London. He, too, was an "unsuccessful competitor"; but the world is better for his life, better for his death, and it may be, better for his failure. General Gordon, too, perishing miserably in that Arab town, waiting for the relief that never came, was an "unsuccessful competitor," but his name shines amid the constellation of the glorious ones who have made our land the foremost on the earth. It is the "unsuccessful competitors" who have glorified this dull old earth, and have made it a good world to live in.

What has made our race the dominant race on earth? It is the magnificent capacity our people possess to be "unsuccessful competitors." They can fight and get licked and fight again, and they never know whether they've been licked or not. Some nations, like the French, can work wonders in an enthusiastic rush; but our nation plods along and gets defeated and plods along some more You can see men on stations holding on, year after year, in spite of floods, and droughts, and fires, and anthrax, and noxious weeds, and vermin, and banks, and overdrafts, and false friends, until they triumph — or die. It is because our race is gritty, and plucky, and tenacious, that it is what it is to-day, and Queen Victoria reigns over the mightiest nation on earth, because her people know how to be "unsuccessful competitors."

The Origin of Tea.

CHAPTER I.

ONCE upon a time, a very long time ago, in the reign of Yuen Ty, in the dynasty of Tsin, there came a strange, sweet-faced little woman into the market place of a famous Chinese town. She carried in her hand a little cup filled with a strange, yellow-tinted liquor. All day long she sold this new drink—which was not wine—to the people, and she gave the money she got for it to the poor and the needy. The curious part of it was that the cup never ran dry, nor ever needed replenishment. It was a marvellous liquor too, for, though it did not intoxicate, it revived and cheered and strengthened all who drank it. The little old woman would tell nothing. She simply sold the liquor, and there was something in it that appealed to everybody's taste. Nobody could tell what that "something" was, but it seemed to meet a craving in life. As the market day drew to a close, the people got terribly excited over the mystery of the cup, and as Chinese are like the rest of us—even though they have to pay a poll tax of £100—they did a very stupid thing. They resolved on seizing the old dame and compelling her to reveal the secret of her cup and her strange liquor. They did so, and put her in jail. When the sun was setting, the old lady rose lightly up in her cell and floated out between the bars of the window, cup and all, and she has never been seen on earth from that day to this, and thousands of moons have waxed and waned since that far off day.

The Chinese missed their chance that time through their own foolishness, and so they didn't find out what tea was for a very long time. It was tea the old lady was selling, and if she had been well treated she would, no doubt, have revealed the secret to the favoured race, but they were too human and foolish. The way tea came to China at last was very curious. There had been a great revival of religion in India for the Holy Bhudda had wandered to and fro in the land, having no place to lay his head, proclaiming the new world's gospel—

"Whereby, whoso will live—mighty or mean,
Wise or unlearned, man, woman, young or old—
Shall, soon or late, break from the wheels of life,
Attaining blest existence.

The disciples of the new faith went out into all the world, proclaiming the gospel taught by Bhudda, and one of them named Dharma went to China. He had been a great sinner in his time, but now, being converted, he was full of holy zeal, and the early days of all new religions are the days of miracles, so a miraculous thing happened to Dharma. He had vowed that he would sleep nevermore, but wander, sleeplessly, all over the earth, proclaiming the great gospel of the universal brotherhood of man. But the flesh is weak, and on a Chinese hill poor Dharma fell asleep. When he awoke he was full of bitterness and woe for breaking his vow. He cried against himself, and he tore out his eyelashes, and cast them on the ground. He swore afresh to sleep no more, and he went out into the world once again with renewed and sleepless vigour.

And it came to pass after many years that Dharma returned unto the hillside where he had slept, and, lo, there grew a strange tree! The eyelashes that he cast to the earth in the bitterness of his sorrow had taken root in the generous soil and had brought forth trees, the leaves whereof were for the healing of the nations. Dharma tasted of the leaves of the tree, and the old weary yearning for sleep that had cursed him for so long passed away, and he became bright, strong and sleepless. Then went he forth, in the midst of the people, selling the leaves of the strange tree, and they gave him welcome, for the story of the old dame who had visited their nation long ago still lingered in the hearts of the people. He was probably a representative of the Atcherley and Dawson of that early day out on the road, but that is a detail. They used to eat the leaves till some clever man learned how to extract the spirit and make the same strength-giving, refreshing beverage as the old woman sold from her inexhaustible cup. So tea became the world's beverage, and the ungracious world has forgotten the origin of the wonderful drink ; but, then, new generations come and go, and each one has sufficient worry of its own to keep it from dreaming of the doings of a past time, and the world is fresh every day to the new souls born into it :

" Fresh buds unclose where withered blossoms grew,
Fresh melodies ring out when skies are blue,
Nature is glad, and the world is ever new."

Some people say that Dharma was a clever Indian tea-dealer, who knew the virtues of the plant he had to sell, and took that method of introducing it into China, but there are sceptics everywhere who cast doubt on all good stories. Let Dharma be what he may, he deserves a monument. People say that in Edinburgh there are two great ones who have no monuments, those are John Knox and Beeleezub, but it seems to me that Dharma deserves a monument from the Australians, as much as either of the aforesaid gentlemen, and if any Australian town wants to ornament itself, and do a good deal, it will erect a monument to Dharma. But I set off to have a long yarn about tea, and tell you all about it in one act, and I can see it sticking out, that it will take a fearful long time, because there are so many good yarns about tea that come tumbling into my mind that there seems no end to them. But I must tell you this ! When I first sat besides a Chinaman in a sampan, on a Chinese river, and saw him burning his joss-sticks before a fat little god made of soapstone, I turned up my boyish nose in haughty scorn. It seemed such a silly religion. But when I found how good and true that little josser was, how tender his heart, and how faithful his life, it broke me up. When, after months of companionship, I had to leave, he gave me a present for my mother in the far away country, and I realised that he was "allee sammee me." That yarn about Dharma introducing tea into China maybe a thousand years before "Christ was born in Bethlehem," stirs strange feelings in my heart. Teamen were as smart then as now, and the great mob was just as credulous, and Dharma made good business, and I don't think one bit the less of him for the good he did the world, even if he did it to his own profit. Tea has become a blessed factor in the world's progress, and the man who teaches the world to drink good tea, and sell good tea, is a benefactor to his race. I remember once—but look here, gossips, this page is nearly full; I'll come back later on, eh?

CHAPTER II.

There were three of us travelling in Morocco—one was a Spanish boy named José, another was a Moslem named Mohammed, and the third was "yours truly." Our horses were good enough to have been Australians, for the way they travelled was perfectly marvellous. They would slide down the banks of dried up rivers, pick their way amongst huge, water-worn boulders, and then climb up some steep bank that looked absolutely impossible for a quadruped. They travelled without food or water cheerily and brightly from "very, very early in the morning O" till nearly noon, when we pulled up at a caravanseri, on the summit of a hill. I never go into such places if I can help it, for insects are fond of me. I was going to Mecca once, as a Moslem pilgrim, and I could have got along first-class, but I couldn't stand scratching. It makes me itch yet when I think of my fellow pilgrims? If dirt meant piety, they were horribly good. But all Moslem caravanseries are past description. They are resting places for travellers. I sent Mohammed in for some tea, and he brought out three cups of warm tea, with no milk in, but, instead, a leaf of green mint. It gave the tea a curious taste, but it was tea, and even with the addition of green mint it was very refreshing. The Arabs drink coffee, mostly, so it came as a surprise, and a welcome one, to get a cup of tea. It is a world-wide beverage and the greatest enemy that whisky has!

It always amuses me to hear teetotallers talking about giving up strong drink, but a man *must* drink something sometimes, and strong drink is often the only decent thing you can get. I've gone into an hotel in the bush to get some refreshment The fellows who drank whisky got it decently served up at once, and sometimes it's decent whisky, but the chaps who want tea—oh, horror! They've got to wait and wait until the kettle boils, and then they get a big dose of bitter tasting fluid in thick earthern cups, with leaden spoons and grimy tablecloths and nameless horrors. I don't wonder that our people prefer to look upon the wine, when it is red, rather than upon tea, when it is black and strong and poisonous. But tea is a good drink if properly prepared; and there are nice tea-rooms starting in all our big towns, where you can get a cup of good tea, nicely served. Tea, well used, is the best friend that the teetotallers have, but it seems to me that they don't use it right. That's a mere detail, but it's an important one. There are houses in this country where you *can* get a good cup of tea, and I have a profound admiration for the people who keep them. They are amongst the world's benefactors, but—

" The best service comes from nameless hands,
And the best servant does his work unseen."

I started off to tell you about tea in China, but
you see how I wander ! It doesn't matter, does it ?
The liquor that was made from the leaves of trees
soon became popular all over China. The Brother of
the Sun, in his palace at Pekin, drank of the refreshing fluid, and so did the humble Chinkie in his house-
boat at Canton Tea came into the life, into the
language, into the very religion of the race, just as
the Nectar of the Greeks and the strong Ambrosial
" Mead " of our Norse forefathers did. Good Chinkies
believe that when a man's body dies his soul does
not die, but goes on in new lives, in strange places, in
other forms. It does not rest, nor pause, nor stay,
until at last "the dewdrop slips into the slimy sea,"
and the human life is mixed with the great soul of
life itself. It is told in the holy books how a wise
Chinaman found out the changes that come to the
soul. It is only when one has attained unto per-
fection, and has joined the passionless, waveless
life-in-death of the just men made perfect, that full
recollection comes. But one Chinkie remembered.
He had died as men die, and his soul had passed
from out this world of ours to that nether world
where the spirits go. Lin—for that was his name—
had lived long on earth and been pretty clever, and
he was greatly interested in all he saw in the strange
world to which he had come. He kept his eyes open.
He had a distinct recollection of what he used to be,
and his mind was all alive as to the possibilities of
the future. The king of the under-world—I've forgotten his name, but he's just about the same as our
Pluto,—was a nice, civil sort of person, and he invited
Lin to have a yarn and a cup of tea. Lin was,
Barkis-like, " willin'," and the tea was handed round.
Just as Lin was going to drink it he happened to
notice that the king's tea was clear as crystal, while
his own was rather muddy. He got an idea in a
moment. The tea he was going to drink had been
faked ! It was faked with " Neponthe," which makes
you forget everything. Once you taste that liquor of

the gods memory fails ! Lin watched his opportunity and upset his cup of tea on the ground, and lived remembering. Then when his soul passed to another body he remembered his career, and that is how the Bhuddists know so much about the other world. Fellows have come back to tell them. They know that—

" While turns this wheel invisible,
No pause, no peace, no staying-place can be ;
Who mounts may fall, who falls will mount ; the spokes
Go round unceasingly."

The charm of getting a reporter into that other would be very great, for his eyes are trained to see, and my impression is that Lin was a reporter, or rather, he was born for one. He did not drink the tea, and he was able to report in the world that lies beyond our ken. None of our reporters ever seem to come back, do they? It's curious. But here's this blooming page nearly full, and I haven't got a good start made yet. Never mind ! I'll hang on to the job - there goes our tea-bell now, and I'm always on hand when the tea is served out.

CHAPTER III.

There are different drinks in different countries, but it is odd to discover that the essential properties of each are very like the others. You drink whisky in the bush—and bad whisky is very bad—you drink Saké in Japan, Samshaw in China, Aguardiente in South America, Pisco in Peru, and firewater of many kinds in different lands. I can't spell all these names, but I've tasted them, so you'll let my spelling go, won't you ? They are all alike in one thing, they intoxicate. There's not such an endless variety of teas, but there's a good many of them. One of the oddest of them all is the South American Maté. I

once had a sweetheart named Candelaria Mayorga
Vaquero, and she lived in Chili. When we had an
evening at home we used to drink Maté　The houses
had no windows to them. You carried the fireplace
out into the street in fine weather, and you kept
it in the drawing room—bed-room and kitchen—in
bad weather. The Maté was boiled in a little black
tin that would hold about a pint. There was a tube
in the tin. It was passed round, and we all took a
suck at it, old and young, toothless and blear-eyed,
young and pretty, dagos and gringoes. When I was
young I did as the Romans did when I was in Rome,
but I never liked Maté. The castanets and guitars
and the gay fandango were all right, and so was the
dark-eyed Candelaria, but Maté, pshaw! That is
about the only really different kind of tea I ever met
with, but the natives drink it because it contains the
essential elements of tea. I'd tell you something
about the way some people make and drink coffee—
the Arabs, for instance—but I'm tired of saying what
I'm going to write. But when I begin to talk about
Candelaria it recalls a fearful lot of yarns that
I'm afraid I'll never get to. Some I'd better never
get to, eh?

> " I have loved, Oh, many a maiden kind,
> 　And many a right good fellow ;
> Where are they all ? So pipes the wind,
> 　So foams the wandering billow."

But I must knock off here to make a remark on
a little story. The Chinamen used to have a mono-
poly of the tea trade, and nobody seemed to know
that the tea tree grew in India. They had lost the
run of it there. About the year 1820, a certain Mr
David Scott was in the northern provinces of India,
and he found a tree that he was sure was the tea tree.
He sent the leaves to the Government Botanist in
Calcutta and asked him to examine them. He did
so, and said that they were the leaves of the
Camelia ! You know that tree, don't you ? Well,
my opinion of botanists is based on that fact. They

are as a class, so full of technical terms that they have very little room for brains, and they dare not be original. I have known a lot of them, and enough good fellows to prove the rule. It's a curious fact that Botany and common sense very rarely grow in the same garden. Poor Scott was set on, and nobody heard any more about Indian tea till about 1834, when another man came across the same leaves, about Kuch Behar and Rangpur. He said: "Camelia leaves or not, these are tea leaves," and, at the point of the bayonet, as it were, he compelled the botanists to admit that tea grew wild in the tiger-haunted jungles of Northern India and Assam.

In 1836 a pound of tea was sent from Assam to England, and in 1840 the great Assam Tea Company was formed; then came a wild boom in Indian tea. This page is too small to give more than a few bald facts, but you can work them out for yourselves, dear gossips. When the Indian tea was discovered there was a rush for tea land, just as there has been a rush to a goldfield with us. Thousands were ruined by it, for there were some curious factors to deal with. First, the tea plant, the great strong, healthy plant of Assam could not stand being coddled and fed, and cared for. It loved the deep, damp jungles, where snakes and tigers and deadly miasmas abounded. It couldn't stand gardens, clearings and delicate attentions, and it pined away. You see, the tree was indigenous to Northern India; that was its home, but it could not stand the new conditions. You take a long, cadaverous bushman to London, and see how sick he'll get. Yet his grandfather may have been a corpulent, turtle-fed London alderman. A generation or two makes a wonderful difference. The way that was met was striking. You can bet your money on a Britisher all the time for getting over a difficulty. I'm proud of my pig-headed race. It's the North Pole business over again. They'll try and they'll die, and new ones will try some more. There is not much sense in trying, but that doesn't matter. If it is

difficult, that is enough   They sent over to China
and learned the tricks of the trade.   They imported
Chinkies, and tools, and all sorts of appliances, and
then they imported Chinese tea plants.   They grafted
the alien Chinkie tea plant on to the Indian native
tea plant, and lo! they had a splendid tea at once.
That filled the bill.   Then the deep valley of the
Assam, where a mighty flood once found its way
through trackless jungles, became a great tea garden,
where thousands of natives, and hundreds of
Europeans lived, laboured, laughed, loved and died.
The tea plantations spread over the land, and when
the coffee crop failed in Ceylon, in 1876, the Cinga-
lese planters tried tea, so that now we have China
tea, Ceylon tea, Indian tea, and, it maybe soon,
Australian tea!   But there was another foe to the
progress of Indian tea that I've not mentioned.   Once
people get accustomed to a certain kind of tea, they
won't take any other sort until their palate has been
educated up to it.   Candelaria and her kindred
preferred Maté to any other kind of tea.   The
people in England preferred Chinese tea to Indian
tea.   The latter was decidedly the best, and
when blended with Chinese tea it beat everything in the world; but the Assamese tea had
this to fight against.   You can't break down the
prejudices of a nation in a day, and we are a conservative gang, all of us.   I see people in the bush
drink hideously black tannin and call it tea.   It
would poison me; but they like it, and they would
laugh my tea to scorn.   This was what the Indian
tea had to contend against, but it won, thanks to the
cunning teamen, who blended the leaves so skilfully
that now we can drink the best tea in the world.   It's
curious how plants of the same kind differ, isn't it?
Yet it is just as Pope says—

" Though the same Sun, with all diffusive rays,
Blush in the Rose and in the Di'mond blaze,
We prize the stronger effort of his power,
And justly set the Gem above the Flower."

A Cheese Mite.

CHAP said to me one day: "I'd write you some news from our part of the country, but there's hardly ever anything happens in the bush." He meant it, too, but that's what makes me laugh. He ought to have said, "I'd write something for the *Stock Journal* only my eyes have never been trained to see." That's the real trouble. Lots of fellows think they could write if there was anything to write about, but the real writer is the one who *makes* something to write about, who writes from within, instead of from without When I've been off in some foreign country as "war correspondent," or on the wallably looking for my tucker, I've seen lots of things. and fellows have said, "Oh, I could write if I were off like that,' but they couldn't, because they couldn't write about the things they saw in daily life. I'd like to have a long yarn with you, gossips, dear, about this writing business, because this office is full of stories intended for the Christmas competition. Some of the writers have the real knack of putting things, and only need practice to become good story-tellers, while others have an idea that all you need to be a story-teller is to be able to "sling English." Some can't even do that. I'd like to be able to read those stories, and then sit down and criticise them, but wouldn't I catch it? Very few people can take a slating in good part. We can't be impersonal and look at things from the outside; we can't see ourselves as others see us, and it's a mighty good job too sometimes. You should hear me getting sat on at times, it would do you good. But what's the odds? I write what I feel and know and think, and I never put on side, and lots of people sympathise with me, so I can stand the other "push" all right.

You wouldn't think that I'd set out to tell you a yarn, would you ? I'll bet you can't guess what I sat down to write! That's the worst of a "Gossip." I sometimes start on a yarn and never get within cooey of it before this page is full ; but it doesn't matter, does it ? What I started to tell you about was cheese mites. My wife won't touch cheese if there's one "jumper" in it, and I'm not fond of live cheese myself. There was a picture in one of the comic papers lately of a "Johnnie" sitting in a restaurant, and saying, with a plaintive look on his face— "Waitaw ! the Gorgonzola has eaten my bread." Well, I don't care for cheese that has to be chained up when not in use ; but the little "jumpers" are curious chaps. I was shipmates with an old skipper once in the China trade, who looked on "jumpers" as the best part of the cheese. He'd rake them all to one side of his plate, season them with mustard and pepper, and then eat them up, smacking his lips, saying, "A fresh mess at sea is welcome." Everyone to their taste, of course, but I don't care for a "fresh mess" of that sort. I'd prefer "salt horse and hard tack," or even damper if I knew the cook. I'm like the chap Dickens talks about—"I likes weal pies ; but I likes to know the woman wot makes 'em." Perhaps it's not well to want to know too much, for it may be true, as the poet said—

"From ignorance our comfort flows ;
The only wretched are the wise."

You get a dozen cheese mites on to a sheet of paper, or on to the dining-room table, and if your soul is attuned to holy things, you'll get as much fun out of them as you will out of the race for the Melbourne Cup. But you've got to be able to see from within, as it were, and illuminate the cheese mite race with the light of your own inner consciousness. If you have a microscope, a steady hand, a

keen eye and a lot of patience—especially patience—
you can see a lot in mites. If you have a low power,
cheap microscope and patience, you can see a lot ;
but even if you have no microscope, but only a seeing
eye and an understanding heart, you'll find a lot of
amusement and instruction in cheese jumpers. You
watch one little fellow. He looks like a white worm
made of rings. He's a bit like an earth-worm, and a
good-sized one is about a quarter of an inch in length.
Now watch him getting along on the soft tablecloth,
or on the paper. You can't see his feet, because "he
hasn't got none." He walks along in grand style, in
spite of that. I had a champion who could do four
inches a minute on a level track. But two inches a
minute is good time. My record is four ! That's
walking, I mean. When they come to jumping they
beat everything, except a flea. But I must tell you
about the walking part of the business first.

We always think that walking implies feet, but it
doesn't. We talk about a ship "walking the water
like a thing of life," and all the feet a ship has are
painted on her stem. The cheese mite has a little
brown horn at the thinnest end of him—which is the
head end—and he sticks that into the tablecloth and
pulls himself along. He does it so quickly that
you'd think he was really walking, but as a matter of
fact his locomotion is caused by a series of pulls,
which are so rapid that his movements look like
walking. He can get over the ground at a good rate,
too, for such a helpless little cuss. But to see him at
his best you must watch him jump. If you have any
sense of humor at all you'll laugh. He has two
funny little suckers on his tail, and when he wants to
jump he stands up on those suckers. Then he
bends his body down and catches hold of his tail with
the little brown beak, flattens his body together, and
jumps clear up in the air. I have seen a champion jump
—24 times his own height. Talk about a circus, eh ?
or acrobats ? Why, cheese mites are clear ahead of anything you ever saw. Fancy having a boy on the

place who could jump his own height clear off the
ground at a standing jump. Why, you'd send him
to Sydney at once. But here's a miserable little
speck of a cheese mite that can jump 24 times its own
height at a standing jump, and then a man tells me
that nothing ever happens in the bush. Oh, pshaw!
I had a champion mite that could jump eight inches
and a quarter; but that was a record. I meant to
tell you a lot more about mites, but this page seems
to get full so mite—excuse me—so soon that you
can't tell much at once. But I'll come back to the
subject later on. Ta-ta, gossips.

There was a wealthy American "lumber-man"
in Sydney lately who was taken to see our beautiful
Botanic Gardens. Some educated people were with
the rich "timber-man," and they went into ecstacies
over the glory and the beauty of the place. He said
nothing until a lady asked him what he thought of
the lovely garden, and then he said, scornfully—
"What do I think of it, eh? Wall, there isn't a tree
in the hull darned place that's worth fifty dollars for
lumber." Exactly. Some people have got lumber
souls, and they never can see beyond trade and
dollars and sordid things. Their souls are atrophied
through want of healthy exercise, and the world,
with all its miracles, all its beauty and grace and
holiness, is simply a place for accumulating money in.
Poor sinners! it's an awful disease to have. It's not
quite as loathsome as leprosy, but if we could see
through shame to reality, we'd recognise it in all its
hideousness, and pity the affected ones.

Some people can admire cathedrals and pictures,
and big, throbbing, powerful engines, but they fail to
see the miracles of daily life and the infinite, unspeak-
able mystery that enwraps such a tiny thing as a
cheese mite. There are those walking in our midst
to-day who are said to be alive, who walk and talk
and act, yet they are dead to every sacred emotion;
they are automatons, money-getting machines, hideous
satires on the great Creator, whose image they are

alleged to bear. There are those in our midst who live in false, shallow, deceitful worlds, who are with us in form, but not in heart, who never think of aught save gold and trade and cunning devices for cheating their neighbours   And there is the one who, as Adam Lindsay Gordon said—

> " Pursues a shadow
> As one who hunts in a dream,
> As the child who crosses the meadow,
> Enticed by the rainbow's gleam "

Ah, me, gossips, we're a queer lot, when you come to think about us, and who of all of you is interested in a cheese mite?

Do you remember my telling you about the tiny brown beak under the cheese mite's head? If you look at that with a microscope of low magnifying power, you'll find that it is composed of two curved bones, which act, as I told you, as a means of locomotion. Between these bones lies the mouth - it does not lie—and when working inside the cheese these claws act as teeth and scrape the food nicely for the hungry little mouth. Close beside the claws, or teeth, or feet, or whatever you like to call the horny little processes, there is the breathing apparatus, and this is an odd little tube built on a marvellous plan I can't stop to tell you about it now, but when the little fellow is stretched out it projects, and when he contracts it is covered with a fold of skin. He has another set of breathing tubes at the tail end, so that when his head is buried in the cheese he can breath through his tail. There's a lot of insects like that, and if I can ever get time I must tell you about them But you can take my word for this, there is more real miracle about a cheese mite than there is about the biggest ironclad afloat, or the finest cathedral in Europe. But we've been educated to look up and away from the lowly things of earth, and my opinion is that if we looked more closely into the things of earth we'd get a great deal nearer to heaven than some of us are ever likely to get under present circumstances

" Aspire not too high,
Although the lark soars to the sky, ·
To utter forth its most melodious sound ;
Still, tis confessed,
It comes to earth to build its nest
Low in the ground."

If you care to watch the history of a "jumper,"
you'll find yourself face to face with one of life's
deepest mysteries. You'll take off your shoes before
the miracle of the cheese mite's life, as a certain one
of old did before the burning bush. If the cheese
mite is not eaten as a " fresh mess," or destroyed by
fire, or cast out to perish in a friendless place, he does
not "die like a dog." Watch him ! Put him under
a fine gauze net, or a glass shade, with some cheese,
and see that it is kept moist, for a mite wants mois-
ture as well as a sheep. In a few days he will stiffen
out and "die." He will lie there hard and dark and
lifeless, and it may seem to you that the processes of
decay, which come to all life, have been set up in
him. But 'tis not so, for Nature, the dear old dame,
is weaving a new pattern from out the putrifying
juices of the cheese mite's body. Life is throbbing
in that dead shell, and when all is ready there will
come a resurrection morn, and a fly will arise from
out the dead matter, to begin a new life, under new
conditions. There is no death. What we call death
is but transition. When the fly shakes off the cere-
ments of the grave, and starts on a new life, it is
gray, and smaller than our common fly. It issues
forth into a strange world, fatherless and motherless,
without experience or education, and yet, borne by
the power which passeth all understanding, it works
out its little destiny, serves its little purpose and
obeys the law, which is more than some of us do. It
mates with its fellows, and seeks for a cheese wherein
to lay its tiny eggs. How does it know a cheese
when it sees it ? Ah, ah ! Step softly, gossips ;
speak low ; you've struck a snag. Let's get away
from that question. The lady gray fly has a tiny

egg-laying tube—they call it an "ovipositor"—and when she has found a cheese she looks for a soft spot in it, or a crack, and then she lays the eggs that will one day be cunning little white jumpers. Then the cheese is carried away and away, and nobody dreams that the tiny eggs are in it, but they are, for " nothing produces nothing " in this world, and you must have eggs before you have jumpers, and you must have gray-flies before you have eggs ; and so goes the weary old world, life and death and joy and woe, and beings' ceaseless tide, and some men say that " nothing ever happens in the bush."

The " Fat Man,"

PARAGRAPH in the *Worker* the other
day set me to thinking. The writer was
kind and generous, and said pleasant
things about our little *Stock Journal* and
its editor, for which, I trust, we were grateful.
Newspaper men are seldom kind to each other in
print; I never could understand why. There seems
to be a fear in their hearts that if they say a kind
word about a contemporary that they will lose a
subscriber, and the other fellow will get a new one.
What a pitiful little spirit that is. I often wonder if
I'm built that way. I don't think so, for I never miss a
chance to say a good word about any newspaper man.
At least, I think so; but we don't know ourselves,
do we? Oliver Wendel Holmes said that every man
is a trinity; there is the man he thinks he is himself,
then there's the man his neighbours think he is, and
then there's the man that he really is. Oh, but we're
a queer lot, and when you begin to try to figure out
what we all are, you get lost in the mists. I think
it would be good for us all just to sit down and
reckon our real selves up once in a while. Most of
us would grow ashamed of our make-up if we did.
But we might come out like Will Carleton's old
farmer, who had written down all the things about
Betsey—

" Maybe you'll think me soft, sir, a-talking in this style,
But, somehow, it does me lots of good to tell it once in a
   while ;
And I do it for a compliment—'tis so that you can see
That that there written agreement of yours was just the
   makin' of me."

But, cronies, that wasn't what I set out to say,
only that chap in the *Worker* set me to thinking,

and I've wandered off the track a bit. He said that
this paper of ours belongs to the "fat men." Is that
you, gossips? It's not me, nor "us," nor "we."
There's no "fat men" in our office, neither literally
nor figuratively. If the phrase stands for injustice,
it's wrong; if it stands for meanness, or mean men,
or hard men, it's wrong. If it stands for unright-
eousness in any sense, it's wrong! This is not a "fat
man's" paper in any sense implied, and it never will
be if I've got a say in making it what it ought to be.
But I believe that the man on the *Worker* who
wrote that paragraph was under a wrong impression,
and I want to have a chat with him, because I think
that he's a good fellow, and does not misunderstand
us wilfully. But these class misunderstandings are a
lot like that story of "Betsey and I are out;" have
you read it? Just consider on what the old farmer
said—

"The first thing I remember whereon we disagreed
Was something concerning heaven—a difference in our creed :
We argued the thing at breakfast, we arg'ed the thing at tea,
And the more we arg'ed the question the more we didn't
    agree."

Well, that's the way with a lot of us in this
world, and what I've discovered is that the alleged
"fat men" are not so very fat after all, and they are
a good deal like lean men, too. There's good and
bad amongst them, of course, but the bad ones seem
to come on top, mostly, in a row. My experience
leads me to believe that there are not nearly so many
"fat men" as there ought to be. Any man who will
go away out into the Never-Never country and take
up a run, who will work it and fence it and ring it,
and make tanks on it, and endure droughts and
floods and fires and ticks and pleuro and liver flukes,
and idle sundowners, deserves to get fat. He deserves
to make his fortune in ten years, and be able to live
the rest of his life in affluence. I've been a good
deal out in the bush, amongst the men who made
this country what it is, and I tell you that if I had

my choice of dying of small-pox in the city and living
in a drought-cursed land, I'd hesitate. This alleged
'fat man" has gone out into the wilds and made the
desert to blossom as the rose ; he has raised the wool
that is the staple product of our country, and has
made closer settlement possible, and what does he get
for it all ? Where are the pioneers who went out in
the early days ? Are they fat ? Not much, my
brother, not much ! How many "fat men " are out
of debt ? How many of them are their own masters ?

When I get out into the bush and find a man
with a nice house and garden and pleasant surroundings, I'm as pleased to see it as if I had a share in
the place, because I feel that he deserves it. When
we can drive to the picnic races, or the show, and
have a good time, I'm glad, because I feel that he
earned it in the flood time, or the drought time, or
the bank-smash time, and I rejoice. But every such
man who has held on to his place can tell you about
hard times and evil days and weary struggles. If he
is well off now, he would have been ten times better
off if he had exercised the same skill, the same
patience, the same energy in the city. When a man
is willing to go on to the land in the Never-Never
country, where the droughts come, and the floods and
the fires, I'd give him the land for nothing. He
deserves it. I'd let him free of all taxation, and I'd
carry his wool free to the seaboard. That would
develop our country. That would reward men for
going on the land. I'd like to see the fat men get
real fat, and grow very rich, because their industry
renders our cities rich.

Do you know what the city dwellers live on, we
non-producers ? We live on extract of "fat men."
We live on the wool and the stock and the produce
that is raised in the country. If we had only coal
and iron and gold to live on, we'd soon grow like
King Midas, and curse the fatal gift that turned all
we touched to gold. We only see the "fat man "
when he comes to the city to spend his money, or at

show-time, when he's having his annual razzle-dazzle, but wait till you see him at work. Wait till you see his grass burning up under the blaze of a merciless sun, and his stock staggering about in the vain search for food and water. Wait till you see him gazing at the steely sky, day after day, looking in vain for the rain-bearing clouds, while the mortgage—the death-grip—is slowly tightening on him. Ah, boys, it's easy to talk about "fat men," to curse them, to tax them and to say hard things about them, but when you come to know them you begin to realise that the "fat man's" life is not all beer and skittles This paper, my "Worker" friend, is not a "fat man's" paper, and I don't suppose it ever will be, but all I want you to do is to disabuse your mind concerning these alleged "fat men." The world is hard to the happiest of us all, and 'tis pitiful that we should throw stones at each other. Far better indeed that we stand together in loving helpfulness to face the inevitable, for, as the Indian sage hath well said—

> Be not mocked !
> Life which ye prize is long-drawn agony ;
> Only its pains abide, its pleasures are
> As birds which light and fly.

How to Learn to Think.

HERE'S a Literary Society in Sydney, of which I'm a member. You'd maybe think that I'd be a bright and shining light in it, but I'm not. There's several people in it who are much smarter than I am, both men and women, especially women! One of their evenings each session is devoted to "Short Speeches on Chance Subjects." The way the subjects are arranged for is this : At the previous meeting, two weeks before, each member writes a subject on a piece of paper. These are given to the president, who delivers them, without selection, to the members present. Some of the subjects proposed are peculiar ; but you take your ration as it comes to you, and make the best speech on it that you know how at the next meeting. Now, gentle gossips, I propose to knock off here and make some remarks about impromptu speaking. You notice how men are often called on to make speeches when they are totally unprepared for it. Well, that's about the most trying position that a self-respecting man can be put into. That man has my deepest sympathy ! It makes me always think of that old Englishman, who said on some such occasion nearly 300 years ago—

> " I know my life's a pain and but a span,
> I know my sense is mocked in everything,
> And to conclude, I know myself a man,
> Which is a proud, and yet a wretched, thing."

My word, especially when you've got to make a speech and don't know what to say when all eyes are fixed on you !

These literary people tried that plan of impromptu speeches, but it didn't work. Very few people can get up on the spur of the moment and make a speech that is worth hearing, especially if the subject is just put into his hands at the moment; so they altered that, and gave you two weeks' notice. Every person, with a sound mind in a sound body, ought to be able to say something sensible on any subject with two weeks' notice, so here's my little say. My question was, "How can a man best learn to think?" That's easy; isn't it? because we all think, we think, without ever having to learn how to do so, but we don't. Do you remember that old conundrum, "Why is Herbert Spencer like a big, hungry dog?" The answer is, "Because he's a great thin-cur?" See! Herbert Spencer is the philosopher of the Unknowable (capital U, printer); he is the synthetic philosopher of the nineteenth century; he is the man who teaches you that you don't know anything, unless it be to know that you don't know anything. He once wrote a book on, I think, Sociology, which shows the difficulties that lie in the way of learning to think straight. It impressed me a lot at the time, and I expect that you could find all my thoughts in other fellows' books, for I don't think that many of us think for ourselves. There was a man named Shakespeare once said that—

"Nothing can we call our own but death,
And that small model of the barren earth
Which serves as paste and cover to our bones."

Before a man can learn to think clearly and freely, he's got to get rid of bias, and if he does that we call him a free thinker, but we make it into one word, and call him a "Freethinker," and that's a term of hissing and reproach. A Freethinker is a bad man, a very bad man, worse than a thief, or a pickpocket, or a forger. There's no hope for a Freethinker either in this world or the world which is to come, and of such is the shibboleth of the blockhead. Yet I've always had a wild desire to be a free thinker, in the honest sense of the word, and to do my own thinking. Most of us put our thinking out, the same as we put our washing. Some get it done in the Methodist Laundry, and some in the Presbyterian. Some patronise the Freetrade Laundry, while some prefer the Protectionist wash-house. But you'll probably put your thinking out to be done for you in the family laundry. That is, you'll grow up and have your thinking done in the family groove. The reason we have so few great thinkers is that we all think in the groove that was made for us ; we're victims of bias from the jump. Of course we don't know it, because we each think ourselves free thinkers, but we're not ! We're tethered to the family laundry. " How can a man best learn to think ? "

Did you ever notice how I stick to my text ? It makes me laugh sometimes when I come bang up against the text I started with. I wander all over creation sometimes and forget where I started ; but I generally turn up the early part of my discourse to see what the subject was. I think that's a compliment to you, gossips, because it shows how much I feel at home in your presence. Some fellows abuse me for being too theological, and some kick me for being too anti-theological ; but there's two points you can bet on me for—one is for always coming back to my text, and the other is for taking up the collection ! Seven and sixpence ! Can't you hear the rattle of the collection box ? But I'm off the text a bit. " How can a man best learn to think ? "

Well, it's easy. First, he's got to learn a good many facts. Now, facts are dry things to get hold of, and plenty of people break down right there. They lack knowledge. You can't get knowledge by intuition. Old Euclid said (or was it Aristotle ?) that there's no royal road to mathematics, so there's no royal road to knowledge. You've got to get filled up with facts first, then you've got to get rid of bias You see, if a man is born in Scotland, he's biassed in favor of Scotchmen. He can't help it. If he's camping down on the Murray, or out on the Paroo, and a fellow comes along and yells, " Hoo's a' wi' ye th' day ? " his heart melts within him at once, and the air grows full of the odour of heather and hills and tatty pats and things like that. He's got a Scotch bias. Look at

me—I'm a Cosmopolitan. I pretend to be above
sectional jealousies and little national biasses, but
I'm not. I'm British, and I think there's no nation
on earth like our own. I preach that "we're a' John
Tamson's bairns," but I mean British bairns. I
mean Australian, or English or Welsh, or Irish or
Scotch, or that push. You see my bias. I can't
help it. I'm sorry for it. I've got good friends in
all lands—French, German, Dutch, Norse and all
sorts—and I think a heap of them, too, but deep
down in my heart I feel sorry for them that they
weren't born under our flag. I'm proud of Britannia,
and proud of her strength and her power—and I'm a
fool therefore—and my heart ever responds to the
words—

> " There's never a flood goes shoreward now
> But lifts a keel we manned,
> There's never an ebb goes seaward now
> But drops our dead on the sand."

Bias, eh? Bias? We're all biassed, and you
can never be a thinker unless you are free from bias.
We're biassed in favour of our own religion, of our
own country, our own politics, and our own race. I'd
like to discuss this point with you, but you can see it,
can't you? Before a man can think freely, and think
correctly, he's got to be free from self-interest, free
from passion and prejudice, and free from the
miserable thralls of this long-enduring bitter stress
that we call life. How many great thinkers have
we? How many great thinkers can we possibly have?
Emerson says, in effect, that the human race is
chimpanzee in pupilage, but as soon as a man begins
to think for himself, he rises above the mass and
begins to control his fellows. But how few rise!
How few think! All we, like sheep, follow a leader,
and our leaders are mostly blind, but fluent, and we
altogether fall into the ditch. My space is full,
gossips, and I don't seem to have properly started;
but it's a good text, "How can a man best learn to
think?"

The Salt of the Earth.

 FEW people went out on a picnic one day recently, and somebody upset the salt. When enough had been picked up to serve the needs of the hour, a genius said, " What is salt?" Then a great hush fell on the company, till one man explained it. He said, ' " Why, salt is—salt, of course." Then a ginger-headed young student said : " I'll tell you what salt is—it's chloride of sodium." That crushed the crowd. They couldn't go back on that, because, don't you see, very few people understand how a man can darken counsel by words without knowledge, or can hide his ignorance with fair phrases which signify nothing. But that is a story by itself! One of the mysteries of my young life was this : How did the sea become salt ? When I grew up I wrestled with the problem. I've been down into great salt mines ; I've stood beside the salt-pans of simple people on the sea shore, and I've wrestled with salts and acids in the laboratory, and—I can't tell you what salt is. But I'll tell you a tale !

Once upon a time, and a very good time it was, a very long time ago, the sea was all fresh water. Nobody needed to take water with them when they went on a voyage. A poor boy lived near the shores . of the fresh water sea, and he loved his mother very dearly, for human hearts have always been the same, and human love has always been an enduring quantity in all the ages of the world's history. This boy, whose name was Peter, wanted to sail away across the mystical sea to some far country to get some of the riches that lie beyond the visible horizon, to bring to his dear old mother. One day a ship came to the shore, and Peter got on board and sailed away into the unknown. But it was a very hard, rough life, and Peter was only a poor boy, and nobody was good to him at all, and the glory of sailing on the sea was not so great as he once thought it was. But after many days they came to a beautiful island, and everybody went to shore to trade. Peter had nothing to trade with, and he was only a sweet-faced, simple ooy, so nobody took any notice of him, for goodness and honesty have never been of much account in this world, unless they were accompanied by other virtues. Peter wandered along the lovely roads and heard the wild birds sing and saw the gorgeous flowers bloom, but his heart was very heavy, for beauty and glory won't fill the place of a good dinner. At last Peter saw an old woman sitting at the door of a poor cottage, and he went over to her and asked if she would give him a drink of water. The old woman saw how tired the poor boy was, and she gave him a drink of water and asked him to sit down. She found that he was very hungry, and she gave him something to eat, and then she asked him about himself. Peter told her all about his dear old mother, who was waiting for him at home, and about his own ambitions and his despair. Then the old woman's heart was touched with tender sympathy, and she said, " I will you something that will be worth more than all the sailors or the captain will ever get, and you can take it home to your mother and live happy all your lives." She went to a cupboard and got out what looked like a little coffee mill, which she set on the table. " Now," said the old dame, " whatever you want you've just got to say, ' Mill, mill, work my will, and grind me out some — ;' and tell it what you want and you'll get it." She then asked him what he would like. He remembered that his old mother was very fond of oatmeal cakes with butter on them, but she was so poor that she could hardly ever get them, and Peter had longed for them very often on

the sea. He asked for some oatmeal cakes with
butter, and the old dame just said, " Mill, mill, work
my will, and grind me out some oatmeal cakes with
butter on them." The mill began to turn, and out
came the loveliest oat cakes that ever were seen,
smoking hot and beautifully buttered. As soon as
enough had been ground the old woman said, "Mill,
mill, you've worked my will, avaunt." Then the mill
stopped. "Now," said the wise woman to Peter, "it
will grind out money, or jewels, or clothes, or anything you want. Take it home with you, but never
let anybody hear you start it or stop it." Peter
went off gladly, and reached the ship, where everybody laughed at the rusty old thing he had brought
back with him.

The ship sailed away, but the wind died down,
and for weeks and weeks the ship lay rolling on the
glassy sea, until nearly all the food was done, and
they were in danger of starvation ; then Peter thought
of his mill. He said to the captain, " What would
you like for dinner to-day ? " The captain said,
" What would I like ? you young wretch, why, I'd
like roast chicken, sweet potatoes and white bread."
" All right," said Peter, and he went into the cuddy,
started the mill, and got all that the captain had
sarcastically suggested. Then the ship was glad, and
Peter was the hero. But he refused to tell how he
got all the things. A breeze came, they reached an
island, and were lying at anchor, when the captain
and the mate resolved on finding out how the boy
procured all the things. They watched him carefully,
and they heard him start the mill, and then they
resolved on a cruel thing. They took the boy, tied
him hand and foot, and carried him ashore and killed
him. Then they up anchor and sailed away. They
laughed and rejoiced over their infamy, and enjoyed
their dinner greatly. The captain said, " Pass the
salt," but there was none, so they agreed to get it
from the mill. They got it out, and put it on the
cabin table. The captain said : " Mill, mill, work

my will, and grind me out some salt," aud the mill started. As soon as the dish was full, the captain said "Stop!" but it didn't stop. He cried, "Hold on; that's enough," but it kept grinding away. Soon the cabin deck was covered with salt, but the mill kept grinding on. Then the cabin began to fill with salt, and still the mill kept grinding on, and the captain grew angry and frightened, and got his sword and cut the mill in two, but each part kept grinding, and the more he cut it the more salt came, and he was nearly smothered in the white floury stuff. He had to go on deck at last, and the ship was down by the stern, and by-and-bye the ship sank with the awful load of salt, and the wicked captain and all his crew were drowned, and the mill keeps on grinding forever and forever at the bottom of the sea, and that is how the sea became salt. That's as good an explanation as any; it's better than "chloride of sodium," but I'll have to quit now, only I'll tell you some more about salt later on. There's one remark I've got room to add, and it's this, and I hope you'll see the connection—

"The spider spins in the furze,
And the dew begems his net;
Fates unseen spindle whirrs,
And the thread with blood is wet."

Poor Peter.

You remember that joke of Darwin's about the relationship between old maids and red clover? Red clover is fertilised by humble bees, which are able to do the work by means of their extra long suckers. If mice are too plentiful they eat the nests of the bees, and the clover will die out. But mice are kept down by cats. Old maids keep most cats, and if it wasn't for old maids there would be no red clover. That isn't all a joke, for it is a solid fact that everything in the world is related to everything else, and the simplest atom in the world is a part of the mighty universe. You get a speck of dust in your eye; that speck may have belonged to a granite boulder, which

was born in a geological convulsion when the world
was young. The history of the speck is the history
of the world. That speck was blown into your eye
by a wind which was produced by a barometrical
depression in the Antarctic Sea, and if you begin on
the wind you reach ultimately that weird statement
that "The wind bloweth where it listeth and thou
hearest the sound thereof, but canst not tell whence
it cometh and whither it goeth." But Russell and
Wragge and that push are doing their level best to
tell us whence it cometh and how it cometh, and all
about it, so where are you? If you try to tell the
history of that speck of dust in your eye you need—

> "All the 'ologies of the colleges,
> And the knowledges of the past."

That doesn't seem to have much to do with salt,
does it? but I wanted you to understand that salt
isn't such a simple thing as it looks. When you go
out into a lonely paddock and find some reddish-
looking rock salt lying there for the sheep or the
cattle—roofed over by careful men - you, maybe,
think you could tell all about it in one act, but I'll bet
you couldn't. My comfort is that nobody can. The
only men who know that they don't know all about
it are the men who have studied the subject more
deeply, while the only men who know all about it are
the men who don't know how little they know.
There's a lot of things like that besides salt. You
ask a man if salt is a good barometer, and he will tell
you "Yes" if he hasn't studied the subject. Salt
gets damp and humid if it's going to rain. I've kept
salt for that very purpose myself, but it isn't true.
Pure salt is formed of a yellow, searching gas called
chlorine, and a bright metallic substance called
sodium. Salt is a chloride of sodium all right; but
the air has no effect on that compound, not the
slightest. But the commonest impurity of salt is
magnesium chloride, and the air affects that. It is
the foreign element in salt that makes the barometer,

but as it is nearly always present, of course the statement is half correct. Now, I want to make a
statement which has nothing to do with salt, but the
subject suggests it as it fits in here. People have
said to me, " I've got a microscope, but I don't think
it's any good, because I can't see live things in water."
Well now, look here, there are no live things in clean
water; it is composed of two gases, oxygen and
hydrogen. When these two gases meet under elec-
trical conditions they make a fearful noise, which we
call thunder, and the water, which we call rain, is
produced. You can take an electric battery and
decompose water into two gases, oxygen and hydrogen,
leaving no residuum, and when you've got them into
separate bottles you can't see anything ; but if you
let them come together you'll get—thunder ? It's a
dangerous experiment, and I once saw a professor
cut himself severely in trying it, in spite of all
precautions. You see the point, don't you ? There's
no life in clean water, and the best microscope will
fail to show you what's not there. Did you ever see
a fellow wander so much ? But if I don't say what I
ought to say to-day, the chance doesn't seem to come
again ! Now for salt !

Along the slopes of the Carpathian Mountains,
there runs a salt deposit. It is over 500 miles long,
it has been proved to be over 100 miles wide, and, in
some places, it is 1,200 feet deep. Now, bring out
Peter's coffee mill, or chloride of sodium, or deposition
by evaporation, or any of your theories you may know
about salt, but when you go down into a mine in
Galicia, you break up. In one of these Galician
mines they have been working for more than six
centuries. But what little impress these human ants
have made on the mighty deposit in all those blood-
stained centuries ! They have hewn out thirty or
forty miles of sunless streets in that vast deposit of
pure salt. They have hewn chapels and images,
saints and shrines, in that under-world, out of glittering, white, glassy salt, and the air has no effect on

them at all, because—the salt is almost absolutely
pure. In the year 1698 these poor Galician workmen
began and hewed out a chapel to St. Anthony, making
the doors, the altars, the ornaments, everything of
pure salt. There the glories of the chapel and the
saints still endure, in the glassy, ghastly, saline air.
Because the salt is so pure, it is not barometric ; it is
not affected by the atmosphere. But fancy living in
a town like that ! If a man was too fresh it would
tame him down, eh ?

How was that immense body of salt deposited ?
What is salt ? Whence came salt ? Here's one
theory. The rivers of earth bring down salt to the
sea. When the fierce sun sucks up the sea to form
clouds, the salt is left behind, and as the ages of
evaporation pass on, the remainder is forever charged
with salt. Aye, master, that is indeed a grand
theory, but we have only moved the problem back a
single step. Where did the salt in the land come
from ? If the great rivers that run through the salt
lands carry their salt to the sea, we can understand
that, but how came the sea salt in the first place if
there was no coffee mill ? As soon as you begin to
ask questions about salt, and lay out the particulars
of the problem, you begin to realise, with Herbert
Spencer, that " The simplest phenomena in their ultimate essence are unknowable." The man at the
picnic who said that salt is chloride of sodium was
very wise, because he was unaware of his own
ignorance, but—I must try and tell you some of the
things I think I know about salt, so I'll see you
later. Ta-ta !

What is salt ? Chloride of sodium ! Salt is the
miracle of life ! Salt is the most marvellous, mysterious,
common combination in all our wonderful world. It
is more valuable than diamonds or precious stones.
We could do without jewels, but thinkest thou we
could do without salt ? Lord Somerville tells a
horrible story about the tortures inflicted on poor
Dutch prisoners in the old long ago. He said : " They

were kept on bread alone, unmixed with salt, as the severest punishment that could be inflicted on them in their moist climate. The effect was horrible, for these unfortunate wretches are said to have been devoured by worms engendered in their stomachs." The horror of that statement is too deep for thinking about, but salt is a good thing. It is like fresh air, pure blood and good health – it is never valued till lost. I often smile at the philosophy hidden in what some people think was a silly remark—"Salt is what gives eggs a bad taste if you don't put any on."

Ah, well, I'd like to tell you how deeply salt is interwoven with this life of ours, how it mingles with our tears, how it is scattered through earth and sea, and starry worlds ; how in one place it is carried in solution, in another place it bubbles from the earth in a brine spring, while in yet other places it forms hills and mountains and solid rocks. And then when you ask a chap what salt is, he sweeps you out of court with a wave of his hand, and shuts you up by saying " it's chloride of sodium." That's the idea— cover up your ignorance with words. I wouldn't mind a bushman, who'd never studied in the schools, saying that, but think of a student, bah! John Ruskin says : " What a boundless capacity for sleep and for serene stupidity there is in the human mind." My word !

But I don't seem to get on with my yarn, do I ? The fact is there's so much to tell, and so little space to tell it in, that it scarcely seems worth while beginning, because you come to the end of the space so soon but I'll hang on now, honest !

If you look at the map of India, you'll see the Runn of Cutch on the north-west coast, away up above the Arabian Sea. Well, that is the great salt mine of India, and the natives used to fight like tigers to gain possession of that part of the peninsula, because it was the real treasure land. They used to make salt from the sea-water on the coast, and if you have a good atlas it will show you how the shallow

seas lent themselves to that. In a hot country like
India they must have salt, and all the animal that is
in the human being—and that is a lot—comes to the
top in the struggle for it. But the Indian salt lake
lies far back from the Runn of Cutch to the south-
east, in the fair Rajpootana, where the Aravulli Hills
melt away into the barren plains. Down in the
valley there lies a lake about 20 miles long and 7½
miles wide in the rainy season. We own that now.
Our Queen took it over for the good of .the natives.
We always do that, you know—for the good of the
natives It was in 1869 that the " Widow " took
over the Sambhar Lake, and between you and me,
gossips, it was a good idea.

If you went out to that lake as the rainy
season was about over, you'd find it one of the
loveliest places on earth. It looks like a sheet of
silver set in a mirror of glorious green to reflect back
the clouds of the day and the twinkling stars of the
dusky night. The green woods are all alive with
the gorgeous bird-life in India. The saline hills are
bursting with young green life. The great rose-
coloured flamingoes, with their brown and white
young ones, wade in the bright waters, engaged in
that far-spread business of picking up a living.
Life is the same on the Sambhar Lake as in Australia,
as far as the deep things are concerned. Life is the
same there to-day as it was 10,000 years ago. The
living things of this spring come and pass, but new
lives come again. There is no death, it is only transition. The wheel of life turns round, or, as the
Indian puts it—

> '' The whirling wheel comes up again,
> And new lives bring new sorrows to be borne :
> New generations for the new desires,
> Which have their end in the old mockeries.''

I must tell you the old Indian legend about that
lake, even if I've got to write another chapter about
salt. You're not in a hurry, are you ? Neither am
I. Well, listen Once upon a time, and a very good

time it was, a very long time ago, there was a holy man lived in a temple, in the beautiful valley of the Sambhar Lake. He was so fearfully good and contemplative that he used to forget his tucker. (I'd like to stop and make a remark on the fact that idle men used to be counted holy men, but I'm telling a tale.) But the gods didn't forget him, for every day a cow used to come to the temple and milk itself into the old man's brass dish, which stood on the floor. One day an inquisitive cow-herd was on the watch and saw the performance, and got a good deal interested. He saw the holy man go to take a drink of the milk, and when he did so he took an amulet out of his mouth and laid it on the carpet. The cow-herd slipped over to the prayer-carpet and put the amulet into his mouth, and he discovered a curious thing. He found that he was taken, in the spirit, to visit every holy shrine in India in a minute of time. I'd like to expand on this subject, but you can think out the fun of that for yourselves. I've got to skip on, for this page is horribly small. That cow-herd was pious, so he took the amulet out of his mouth and restored it at once to the holy man. Honesty must have been as rare then as now, for the old gentleman was so pleased that he rewarded the honest fellow. He sent him to the goddess Sumtra Deva, who made him a horse and told him to ride eastward on his steed and never look backwards. You remember Mrs. Lot? You remember Orpheus and Eurydice? Well, the Indian josser was the same. The poor cow-herd set off, and I'll bet he meant all right, but as he rode under a tree he lost his turban That was easy enough, and he looked back for it, just as you'd do yourself, and that ruined him. The horse wouldn't go any further, and the cow-herd was done for. He just had to start and walk back, and lo! it turned out that if he had gone travelling east for long enough all the world would have been covered with gold and silver, for the Sambnar Valley was that now. The wise men knew that if gold broke out that way there would be a "rush," and the place would be pegged out at once (this was millions of years ago, you know), and they didn't want that. The wise men of Rajpootana asked the cow-herd to go and request Sumtra Deeva to take back her gift. She did, just like a spiteful woman. Instead of turning it back to the green woods and flowery meads, as of yore, the jealous old cat made it into a bitter salt land, and that's how the Sambhar Lake came to be what it is to-day. But I'll tell you some more about the lake another time.

When you travel out into the bush after a good healthy rainy season, and watch the wild flowers springing up on every side, you think what a glorious country Australia is   You almost envy the fat sheep and lazy cattle that have such boundless stores of feed. You do envy the squatter who owns the broad, fat lands and the countless flocks and herds, and you wonder how it comes that wealth and happiness are so unevenly distributed. But, perhaps, you may come at another time, during a weary drought, when no green thing is visible on the face of a scorched earth ; when the air over the paddocks is full of dust ; when there is not a drop of water to moisten your parched tongue, and Dante's Inferno rises to your mind. You will see dead sheep and cattle everywhere, and hopeless, dispirited men   You will hear of mortgages and overdrafts, of a fearful death rate amongst the cattle, and of the despair of the men on the land, because the skies are brass. Then you think it would be better to be a member of Parliament than a "bloated squatter.' Well, the Sambhar Lake is the same way.

After the rainy season it is a picture of loveliness. The birds sing in the trees, the young green shoots of verdure cover the hillsides, and the shallow lake is a picture. But there comes a few hot days, a few hot winds, and the glory of the lake fades away. 'Tis only a superficial beauty. The flowers and grasses fade and die beneath the fierce Indian sun, the birds depart, and the valley becomes the most hideous in Rajpootana. The hills grow gray with a saline deposit that seems to exude from the earth, and the shallow lake begins to dry up. At its greatest depth it is only about four feet deep, and there are miles and miles of it that are even less than that. Fancy a shallow lake like that in one of our Western plains! We have them, too, but they are not charged with salt as this one is. When the sun has sucked up the water it becomes one vast bed of glittering white salt, from two inches to less in thickness. Here and there are black pools of brine that are deeper than the rest, but they, too, will be evaporated at last by the power of the fiery-eyed god of day.

You know what salt is, don't you? We all know? Everybody knows what salt is! But if we've wrestled with the problem at all, we soon find out that we don't know, and this salt that crystallises on the bed on the Sambhar Lake reveals itself to us as the great mystery of nature. This salt comes from the hills and the land about, and it crystallises on the black mud that forms the bottom of the lake; but to see it crystallise is a miracle. Salt crystallises in cubes. Everything in the world has a form of its own, but the science of crystallography is too deep to wrestle with here. All I'm going to do is to stop and make a remark about crystallisation as seen through the microscope. Take a glass slide, warm it slightly, then rub it with salt water and put it under the microscope, and you'll see Nature working her miracle! It will freeze, as it were, on the warm glass. Better still, take some Epsom salts and rub the liquid on the glass and watch the crystallisation. It beats all the shows you ever were at. You see the ways of the dear old dame who rules the universe, and if your soul is sufficiently illuminated to see the miracle you'll hold me to be your friend for evermore. John Oliver Hobbes says: "To be wilfully honest with another human being for even half-an-hour is enough to establish some claim, at all events, to an immortal soul. Well, if you watch old Nature at her work of crystallisation for half-an-hour honestly, you'll know whether you've got a soul or not.

I set out with the firm determination to tell you about the Sambhar Lake, in Rajpootana, and see where I've got to, but what's the odds? I've thought of a whole lot of other things that I must tell you about, and this is the last yarn about salt, and I don't care whether I get finished or not, so there! The salt crystallises on the soft black mud of the lake, and the natives wade in the mud and lift it off. They lay it in little heaps, all the way along, as they travel, until they have skimmed all the salt off the lake. Women then come with little baskets and carry the piles to the shore. The Government officials receive it at the stores, which may be several miles distant, and they weigh and measure what is brought in. They gather as much as 100,000 tons of salt in a season from the Sambhar Lake, so you can guess the enormous value of such a salt lake in the olden times. No wonder the Indian tribes bathed the shores of the lake in blood to obtain possession of it. But it belongs to Queen Victoria now, to the Widow of Windsor—

> "We've bought her the same
> With the sword and the flame,
> An' we've salted it down with our bones.
> Poor beggars, it's blue with our bones."

The salt crystallises on the surface when the water evaporates, but the cruel little crystals form in the mud as well, the heat of the sun works down into the mud, and the crystals form then. When the bare-footed natives wade into the mud, the crystals tear their human skin, and the poor dusky swimmers come out all bleeding and scored. Then the merciless Indian sun shines down on them, and it looks as though life were not worth living. Yet these dark children of the Indian land are our fellow subjects. They are part of the Widow's kingdom, simple, gentle, patient creatures, who are as human as we Australians are. Think of the life they had at places like the Sambhar Lake! Poor souls, Queen Victoria has come to bless them, for a railway runs to Sambhar now, and the vast salt deposits are carried far afield by the iron horse, but life is still hard and cruel to them. I'd like to tell you some more about salt, about why it is unlucky to spill salt at the table, and a lot more things, but I've said too much already, and I pray that—

> "Through the naked words and mean
> Ye may see the truth between."

When I saw that salt spilt at the picnic, and heard that salt was "chloride of sodium," it filled me with woe. I wanted to tell you about Galicia, Sambhar, and the salt mines of Cheshire, but, somehow, I talk too much, for I'm afraid of piling up facts in too solid a mass. But I fear that my facts get diluted too much, yet, gossips, you bear patiently with me, and I'm grateful, but I must not trespass on your good nature. I'll try and not worry you with science, yet I do want tell you of the things that have filled my own life and widened my my own horizon. All I can say is, that I'd like you all to think on the subject we gossip about, and then you will become "the salt of the earth."

Breeding Human Beings.

was making a passage in a steamer once upon a time, when the yellow fever broke out in our midst. We had picked up the foul disease in Aspinwall, on the Isthmus of Panama, or else in Jamaica, but nobody seemed to care much where we got it —all that we were certain of was that we had got it. The chief engineer was the first to die, and we sewed him up, and had a quiet little funeral service over him at midnight. We stopped the ship to slip him overboard, but that alarmed the passengers, so we never stopped for another funeral. When a man died we sewed him up in canvas, with a few grate-bars at his feet for sinkers, and laid him aside till it grew dark and the passengers were asleep, then—we gave the dead one his passage over the side.

When we sat together, the rest of us, with a "deader" or two hidden away, we used to discuss every subject under heaven except—yellow fever. That was the subject that lay the nearest to all our hearts ; we didn't know whose turn would come next, and, being human, we were sore afraid, yet we spoke not of our terrors to each other, but rather, each man tried to cheer his neighbour by appearing unconcerned. You and I, gossips, are like the men on that ship ! We have thoughts that are too deep for utterance ; we think things that we may not speak ; we muse on matters that we may not discuss, and yet we are fools for not speaking out, but who among us dares to bell the cat ? And how may we speak ? Was it not Longfellow who said ?—

> " I wonder if ever a song was sung
> But the singer's heart sang sweeter?
> I wonder if ever a rhyme was rung
> But the thought surpassed the metre ? "

A long time ago, dear gossips, perhaps a year ago, I had a gossip with you on the subject of breeding human beings. I said that we in Australia breed the best sheep in the world, and we breed, also, some of the meanest human beings. And we do, don't we? The reason is simple. We apply the rules of common sense to the laws that govern the propagation of domestic animals, but we leave the perpetuation of our own race to chance, to passion, to crime, to infamy, and to ignorance. The men who sat on the hatch on that steamer with a couple of corpses near to them, yet never discussed yellow fever, were wise, were manly, were heroic compared with us. We are fools and blind, wrapped up in social habits that enslave us, bound in hideous old superstitions that curse us, and kept back from social freedom and world-wide happiness by our bestial ignorance.

When I dared to touch on the subject of breeding human beings, there arose in these columns a bitter controversy on the subject of education, which was carried on under the heading of "Breeding Human Beings;" but it was a farce, masters, a farce, for nearly all the writers missed the point. Yet the discussion was valuable as showing how the words had stirred thoughts, and men wrote to me about the article from the uttermost ends of the earth. One large-souled man, writing from Chicago, U S.A.—a man I had never seen or heard tell of, the editor of a great paper—said, "A doctor's certificate should accompany a marriage license." Exactly, neighbors; that's the very idea! But, if you want to know what a solid grip Mrs. Grundy has on us all, you dare to mention the subject to nice people, especially to nice, pious people, and you'll get crushed. You'll be made to feel yourself a fool, if not a knave.

Listen. I knew a family in—well, never mind where—that had broad-shouldered, pure-blooded sons. They were a magnificent lot of people. One of the sons fell in love with a pretty woman who came of

evil stock. There was drunkenness, scrofula, and
crime in her family. The old settlers on the river
knew her record, and shook their heads at the
marriage. They knew how Nature works, and they
understood that, though the woman herself was
bonnie and bright, sorrow would come to her children,
for Nature will not be contemned of any. She visits
the sins of the fathers on the children, even unto the
third and fourth generations of them that strive to
walk uprightly. Yet not a soul dared to raise his
voice in protest against the union. Not a man dared
to say aloud what he thought in secret, or even what
he whispered to his fellows. Yet the deep, awful
blight of heredity followed that union, and the earth
was cursed with woe because of it. Children were
born into the world to bear the curse of evil deeds
done in the long ago. Poor, frail, feeble bodies were
endowed with life, and they in turn conveyed the
blight to others, and the evil currents of the " love
match " are flowing to-day through the earth.

People look pityingly on the sick ones and
murmur something about "God's will," as though God
had sent trials of this kind on earth, as though God
were cruel, unjust, merciless, horrible. No mortal
man could conceive a demon more dreadful than the
God some orthodox people figure to themselves
with the smug approval of their ignorant but well-
meaning neighbours. No wonder that our gaols,
hospitals, poor-houses are full to overflowing; no
wonder that we are cursed with idle, vicious good-for-
nothings. We try to educate them, to enlighten
them, to " convert " them. We put them in gaols
and reformatories, and weep over them, aye, we pity
them, but we dare not so much as hint at the source
of the evil, because we say, in our blind folly, that
" God sends little children," and we say, too, poor
fools that we are, that little children are born into
the world with pure minds, ready to have the characters of their surroundings written on them. It's a
lie, false, shallow, pitiful, born of our own dense

ignorance. The man is the outcome of the lives of those who went before him, and the Hindoos grasped a magnificent truth in that strange statement that

> " Each man's life
> . The outcome of his former living is ;
> The bygone wrongs bring forth sorrows and woes,
> The bygone right breeds bliss."

You say we cannot mend things. No, we cannot, until a sufficient number of us dare to make our voices heard in the world—and we will, too, but not much in your day nor mine, gossips. We die, but the race goes on ! Some day men will awaken to the awful truths of heredity, and they will cry for social reforms compared to which freetrade, protection, land tax and kindred matters will be as naught. But we must stumble blindly on through the years of gloom and sorrow, waiting for the age of sense to dawn on a bestial earth. Did you ever insure your life ? How they enquire concerning the ages of your relatives and the cause of their deaths ! How they enquire about the character of the diseases that afflicted them all, and if you make a false return your insurance will be declared null and void. Some day, when men are wiser, such a certificate will be required on the altar, and if any parson marries a couple. without a clean record, then he will be dealt with as Nature deals with incapables. But we are a long way from that yet, because we are fools and blind ; yet am I comforted in fighting, because that wise man in Chicago has heard my cry in the *Stock and Station Journal*, and has written to say that " A doctor's certificate should accompany a marriage license." Gossips, we have but touched the fringe of this awful question. Some day, if life and strength are spared, we'll come back to it, eh ?

The Slave of the Pipe.

HERE Jwas . once a man who was badly afflicted with his eyes. The doctor was called in and prescribed for him. In giving instructions to the patient, the doctor said : " Do you smoke ? "   " Yes, heavily." " Well, you must give up smoking at once, and I'll call back in a week." At the end of a week they were still bad ; at the end of three weeks they were still bad. Then the doctor asked, " Are you sure you have given up smoking ? "   " No," said the patient, " I have not." " Then," said the medico, " you must say good-bye to your eyes." Then the poor man heaved a deep sigh, and said, " Good-bye, eyes." Then the band played, and men who loved their pipes sympathised with the sick fellow. Better to be a beggar boy with an appetite than an old, rich man with the gout. Better to be young and strong, and able to enjoy your pipe, than to be old and wise and unable to smoke. Better be — but that's enough. The men who smoke can fill in the rest, and the folks who don't smoke can't understand.

Dear gossips, excuse me for knocking off a minute to have a yarn. If nobody but the people in the bush read this page, I'd tell you lots of little yarns about what I think and feel and do, but you can't keep other people from reading it, and I don't want to take all the world into my confidence. If we put a big notice on top of this page, " For bush people only," you'd have all the rest reading it, and that's just what we don't want. That's the feeling I have, and I'd like to be able to get over it. Then, too, it's not easy to say what lies deepest in your heart when you know you'll meet some chap in town

some day who'll say, "Hello, 'Gossip.'" There are
very few of us wear our hearts on our sleeves, and
we don't like to let people know exactly what we
think, do we? I tell you, it's awfully hard to be
honest in this world. It's just as Omar Khayyám,
the Persian poet, said—

> " 'Tis but a day we sojourn here below,
> And all the gain we get is grief and woe,
> And then, leaving life's riddles all unsolved
> And burdened with regrets, we have to go."

I knew a man in Sydney that I always looked
upon as a man with no sorrow. He was a Bohemian
chap, clever, big-hearted, easy-going and tolerant.
Perhaps he was a bit too thoughtful for a real
Bohemian, because sometimes when I'd meet him he'd
look very serious; but as soon as he saw me the
clouds would flee away, and the genial soul would
shine through his eyes. Occasionally we'd adjourn to
a restful place for a little spiritual refreshment and
have a quiet smoke and a yarn, and we'd enjoy it,
too. You see, when everybody is liable to read this
page, you don't like to say things of that sort, for if
you're a writer you've got to pretend to be better
than common people. But you know me now, dear
gossips, don't you? You know I'm only human and
made of clay, and just like the rest of the crowd,
don't you? Still, we don't like saying things out
too loud, for fear of the fellows who are not in
sympathy with us. Well, one day recently I met
my friend, and we had a pleasant little spell, and
were just parting, when he dropped a word or two
that gave me pause His life was *not* a happy one.
His pleasant smile but hid a sad heart; his genial
ways covered a weary spirit and a broken life.

Then we come back to the old, old story—can
you read your neighbour's heart? Do you *know* the
people you rub shoulders with every day? Ah, boys,
every heart has its own bitterness; every life has its
own shadow; every cupboard has its own skeleton.
We say things like that, all of us, but we don't

realise them. We think we mean them and understand them, but we don't. Some day, riding back from the service at a graveside, we catch a glimpse of a laughing face, and we wonder how the world can laugh when our sunshine has faded. Yet, oftimes, men and women can say, and say truly, " Death is a sweet sorrow compared to my woe." When my friend spoke I realised with a crushing force how little I knew of his life. A cruel, horrible disease was eating his life out. I cannot tell you, gossips, dear, how I came to understand the nature of that disease, because of the reason I gave you before, but I knew I could cure him if he were willing to pay the penalty and to endure the privations that must come. I said to him that "Life under such conditions is not worth living," and he moaned bitterly, " No, indeed."

My friend was willing to do all that was necessary, except to give up his pipe and tobacco ; it was very nearly— " Good-bye, eyes." Life is hardly worth living to some men if they can't smoke and drink ; yet life is sweet and pleasant unto each when it comes to a clinch. Said I, " You can't get better if you smoke and drink " Said he, " It's all very well for you to talk, but you can't realise how much it means to me." Then remembered I a great man, whose name was Paul, who, on a certain time, said : "Wherefore, if meat make my brother to offend, I will eat no flesh while the world standeth, lest I make my brother to offend." That seemed a high standard to reach to ; but I said, " Friend, if you will give it all up, I will also." Then he looked me straight in the eye, and, after a brief pause, he took my hand and said, "So be it." And now I'm just thinking what a fool I've been through the weary years. I had no idea that there was so much pleasure to be had out of a simple Pauline act. I smoked too much to be good for me. You could hardly see across my office sometimes for smoke. Now I'm saying to myself—

" Tobacco is a noxious weed,
It was the devil sowed the seed ;
It drains the pocket, soils the clothes,
And makes a chimney of the nose."

My opinion is that it's easier to give up both smoking and drinking rather than one of them. I know a man in the bush who goes to town and says, " Now I'm going to keep straight ; only two whiskies to-day." But the first whisky weakens his resolution, and the second washes it all away, and when he gets home he sees two trees where only one grows. A man who does a thing like that over and over again has less sense than a horse, or a dingo, but there's a lot of men keep on at it. ¡Some of us can take a refresher at times, and leave it alone when it's likely to get to be the boss ; but a chap who can't do that should give it best entirely. That's why I think the only safe way is to chuck it altogether. But if you hang on to smoking you must have a drink—at least, most of us must, and if you hang on to whisky you're sure to smoke if you know the way, so if you're going to reform you've got to do it solidly.

Did you ever hear of a boy whistling as he walked down a dark road at night to keep the ghosts away ? Well, I expect that's me ! I'm trying to screw up my courage to stand by what I know is the right thing. But I'm a poor, weak sinner, and I've written this to pin my resolutions down and take you into my confidence, gossips, dear. Will any of you boys come and join me ? Will you chip in and hold my hand while I walk without a smoke, or a " nip," eh ? I would not say this only I've found out that so many of you are human and kindly and helpiul, and I want to do the square thing myself. What do you say ?—

" Of your gladness lend a gleam
Unto souls that shiver ;
Show them how dark sorrow's stream
Blends with hope's bright river."

Grandfather's Clock.

E sat on the Lookout at Katoomba, talking about fat stock, for men will talk about their business even on the steps of the altar. When the glory of the scenery finally overcame the market prices, we sat gazing on the mystic blue haze of the lone mountain ; on the panorama of hills rolling away to the sky line where the blue of the earth and the blue of the sky became one. I said to Steve, " What makes these mountains so blue ? " He said, " Oh, it's an atmospheric effect due to the extreme tenuity of the air," and he was satisfied. He had covered his ignorance with a brave show of words, and felt as if he had explained things ! Over at the Ruined Castle, on the other side of the valley, there were miners lying on their sides, in long, low, dark passages, cutting out blocks of kerosene shale for a pitiful little wage. I asked Steve what kerosene shale was, and—he gave it up. Nobody knows what it is, nor how it came to be where it is, but men like Steve can explain all about the blue haze. Why miners should have to work in such soul-destroying dirt and darkness for starvation wages, in the midst of the blue haze, is the kind of a problem men like Steve can never solve.

When we got back to the weatherboard shanty that we lived in at Katoomba, we found Steve's father moaning helplessly on the little bed on the inside room, where he had lain this many a day. He was only 70 years old, but he was dying of old age. Poor old soul, he had led a hard life in his early days in New South Wales, and he was worn out at seventy. As he lay moaning softly in the still afternoon, little Steve, his grandson, came creeping softly up to me with a picture book in his hand. I opened the book, and looked at the pictures of the Ark, and of utterly impossible, gorgeously-coloured Shems, Hams and Japhets, and then, somehow, got to teaching little Steve his alphabet. The old man lay softly moaning out his life, finished with all its turmoils, weary of all its joys, and here was his grandson just beginning life, but not one whit wiser for the old man's deep experiences. The grandfather's struggles, groans, tears and triumphs were as nothing to the small boy. He would die and take his knowledge to the grave, and the child would have to begin life for himself, even as he was now learning his letters.

That night the old man died, very quietly, just as poor men have learned to die I have stood at the side of men dying, in all lands and climes, on sea and shore, in calm and storm ; they have died of cholera and consumption, of yellow fever and senile decay ; but, somehow, I've never seen any fuss about it ; they go out into the dark very quietly. The fuss is made by the fools about them. When the crowd came to the funeral they looked sad and sympathetic, and they behaved themselves very respectfully, and when the hearse—we had a hearse—moved off down the bush road to the far-away cemetery, they looked liked a lot of patient, ignorant plodders who had listened respectfully enough to the parson, but still felt unsettled in their minds, like—

" Poor pitiful pagans, who didn't know
When they came to die where their souls would go."

When Steve came back from the funeral he told us where the old man had gone to. Heaven was like the blue haze on the mountains. It was all clear to Steve. No astronomical difficulties troubled him. Heaven was "up there." When his father's father had died in England he went "up there"; but he went in the opposite direction to the old man who died in the Blue Mountains, for he lived at the other side of the world, and the world is round, so if they both went up where would they meet? You know

54   *Australian Gossip and Story.*

all about it till you begin to think about it. Steve
thought he knew all about it, but, then, he didn't
think about it. He " believed."

The day after the funeral there was a terrible
hailstorm, and the ground was fairly covered with
the icy bullets. It stormed all day long, and the
children of the house said, " Can't you make grandfather's clock go ? " It was a queer little, old-
fashioned clock in an iron case, that stood on the
mantle shelf. The old man used to oil and dust it,
and wind it up, and fool with it for years before his
death, but it hadn't been going for many a day. I
said I'd try, as I was stormbound ; but I didn't know
any more about clocks ¡than Steve knew about
the blue haze, or about heaven ; but, then, I knew I
didn't know, and Steve didn't know that he didn't
know, and that was the difference.

I took the clock down, took off the face,
unhooked the pendulum, and lifted the works out of
the case ; that was easy ! Then I loosened it all,
but if I had taken it to pieces I could never have put
it together again. After oiling it all, and shaking it
a good deal, I screwed it up, returned the works to
the case, put the face on again, and wound it up ;
but it wouldn't go. I took it out again, examined it
closely, and found that one brass plate had been
screwed up on the wrong side of another brass plate,
so I started to loosen the blessed thing to get those
pieces into their proper place—and all the while the
children watched me with anxious eyes. They
thought I was clever, and I tried to look so. The
clock was loosening beautifully, and I could almost
get the two brass pieces into their right places—
another shake and another pull would do it— when,
WHIRR ! there was a wild, blood-curdling shaking in
my hand, and the blessed clock seemed to fly into a
million pieces ! The spring had been wound up since
I had put the confounded thing together, and that
had unwound itself with diabolic glee, and had
jumped out of my hands with a kind of quivering

mirth, and rolled away under the sofa. I never moved a muscle, but tried to look as though clocks always acted that way. Then the little ones gathered up the fragments, and kept bringing me more wheels and more wheels, till it seemed that the accursed clock was like the man whom the murderers cut up to carry away. They said they had no idea there was so much of a man! I put the clock together, but, when screwed into the case, I had five wheels too many, so I dropped them into the case, and said it was probably out of order, and that was why it had not gone for a long time. Next morning I took the train for Sydney, but that clock has taught me a lesson! Steve knows as much about heaven and the blue haze as I know about clocks; and, when you come to think about it, nobody knows much about anything after all, and the wisest man is, perhaps, the man who knows that he doesn't know much.

Kesher Meat.

N the Book of Leviticus it is written that "The blood is the life of all flesh ; the blood of it is for the life thereof; therefore, I say unto the children of Israel, ye shall eat the blood of no manner of flesh ; for the life of all flesh is the blood thereof ; whosoever eateth it shall be cut off " Strange it seems to visit Glebe Island Abbatoirs and watch the working out of that old commandment in the nineteenth century amongst the Hebrew people. The odd part of it lies in the fact that modern science is fast bringing us to the position occupied by Moses thousands of years ago. We stole the religion of the Jews, improved (?) on it, and killed the Jews for not accepting our improvements, for if we accept the Mosaic theory about killing cattle, in this enlightened age, then we may as well admit that the Jews are not altogether fools Moses was the clearest headed man of his age, and we have not yet fully realised how clever he was. He belongs to that small class—

> " Who stamped the signet of their souls so deep
> In art or action, and whose memories keep
> Their height like stars above our misty ways."

Moses affirmed that it was bad to eat beasts which had not been bled. To that we all agree, but our butchers stun the cattle with a blow, or else pith them in the vertebral column, in such a way that a sudden change is set up in the blood by the cessation of the heart's action. The Jew, at Glebe Island in the month of May, 1894, lives up to the law of Moses, and refuses to have his beasts killed in that way. Every joint that goes to a good Jew's table must come from a beast that has been properly bled. So the Jew butcher is not a simple tradesman, selected from the ranks by advertisement or favoritism

—he is the *Shochet*, appointed by the chief Rabbi of England for the service of the sons of Abraham in Australia. The business of this Shochet, or killer, Mr. P. N. Philipstein, is to inspect the cattle for Hebrew use, to kill them, to inspect them after killing, and to stamp all meat that passes his inspection with the stamp of his office " Kosher right.

THE " KOSHER " MARK.

This stamp signifies several things. It means, first, that the meat is healthy, with no sign of disease about it. The Shochet will not pass a sheep with the slightest sign of "liver fluke" about it. He will not pass a cow or calf with the faintest trace of tuberculosis about it. The meat must be, like Cæsar's wife, above the shadow of suspicion before the " Kosher " stamp is placed upon it. The mark on the beast signifies, too, that it has been properly bled according to the old Hebrew fashion, and that whoever eats it does not eat with it the blood "which is the life thereof." Strange it seems that this custom of the Hebrew people should have endured longer than any kingdom on earth. Noble nations have slowly risen, reached their prime, and slowly perished, but the custom of the Hebrew Shochet has failed never. The Jews have been the most sincerely hated and most bitterly persecuted race on earth, and have been hunted like beasts through long ages, but they still cling to their "Kosher" meat, and the reason is not far to seek. A great teacher has said that "No reform is worth its cost which is not important enough to rise to the level of a religious duty. Make it that to the consciences of men, and it will live; make it less than that, and men will play with it for a day, but will never build it into anything that will live for future ages." The Jews made the killing of beasts part of their religion, and a good system has endured from Sinai to Glebe Island, and that is a good stretch!

The Shochet of to-day is provided with excellent tools. He carries his long-bladed, razor-like knives in handsome cases. They are the implements for a religious service, not the tools of an artisan. He takes a becoming pride in his duties, and he has a right to do so. If we are justified in being proud of a piratical grandfather, who enriched the family by proceedings which will not bear investigation, surely the Shochet may well be proud of his trade, which was founded by Sinaitic thunders when the world was young.

When a beast, say a calf, has been approved of by the Shochet, it is secured round one leg by a rope, and a pulley raises the ill-fated animal off the ground by the one limb. Another leg is secured, the beast's head is bent back—generally by a Christian – and the sharp knife of the Shochet does the rest; and if the Christian world could look on the sight would shock it. The blood, certainly, escapes through the gaping aperture, and the Mosaic law is strictly adhered to. We apologise for intruding this ghastly business on our gentle readers — all readers are "gentle"—but we may be excused for recalling that exquisite little French story about a butcher :—A lady said to him, in horrified tones, "Oh, dear, yours is a very dreadful business · killing the poor little lambs." Whereat the simple butcher, in great surprise, ejaculated, "Bless me, madame, do you want to eat the little lambs alive?" We may shut our eyes to the slaughtering business as long as we eat meat; but, unless we "eat the little lambs alive," or take to vegetables, it must be done.

After the beast is properly dressed by the butchers, the Shochet examines it carefully, and if there is anything suspicious about the carcase, it goes to the Christians. We have no religious scruples about our beef or mutton, and so we can afford to eat what the Jew would reject. If we rejected all that the Shochet rejects, we would never enjoy a pork chop or a rasher of bacon, so we may be allowed to cling to our own ways. If the beef, or mutton, or veal passes the Shochet, he stamps it all over. You could not cut a joint from a beast without a stamp upon it; you could not cut a chop from a sheep without part of a stamp upon it, so that the Hebrew knows, when he buys a joint of meat, that it is "Kosher" right, that it is healthy meat, and has been bled in Mosaic fashion.

This mark is made with a vegetable compound, and is perfectly innocuous and enduring. The beef may be corned or salted, but when it comes out of the pickle, there is the "Kosher" mark still upon it, so that there is no trickery possible in the "Kosher" meat trade. Now comes the little joke. The Jews buy their "Kosher" meat mostly at Buttel's, in Pitt-street, who are not Jews, but they are good butchers. The atmosphere round our beautiful harbour has a corroding effect on most religions (except picnicking), and many of the Jews have given up "Kosher" meat, and use the ordinary beef of commerce, the common sort that we eat ourselves. This spoils the trade, because unless all the Hebrews eat the specially prepared meat, there is no trade for a "Kosher" shop. But there is a law of compensation at work, for many Christians, especially medical men, will have nothing else but "Kosher" meat; so that, in spite of Hebrew defections, the butchers do a good trade, and the marked meat is always on sale. So

do things change!   The larger liberty the Jews
enjoy is loosening the old bonds, and they are eating
of luscious Christian meat, in spite of Sinaitic
thunders.   The Christian hatred of the Jew is—in
New South Wales at least — a thing of the past, and
so the Christian is eating Jewish meat, and we are
gradually drawing nearer to each other, but we may
adopt the Hebraic institution of the Shochet with
much benefit to our system, and the Jews may, with
equal advantage, come to partake of many of our
Christian dishes now forbidden to them, because, in
spite of ancient ordinance, they are really " Kosher."

The Consumption Horror.

ORE than 3,000 human beings die every year in Australia from consumption! No brilliantly-illuminated horror could possibly be more appalling than the bald, simple statement. It should be written in letters of fire across the portal of every church, meeting-house, and business place in the land. Men ought to understand the full horror of the proposition, and then, perhaps, we would take some strong measures to stamp out the disease, for it can be stamped out, now that we know what it is and how it is caused, nursed, developed and disseminated; but we never seem to wake up to the facts of the case. When the " Victoria " goes down, and 500 lives are lost, all the world thrills with horror. When a thousand soldiers lay dead on the battlefield, every kindly-hearted human being shudders at the slaughter; but more than 3,000 people die every year in Australia from this insidious, accursed and preventible disease. In our lovely climate, with all our bright sunshine and pure air, we sit down with folded hands before this awful disease, and yet—we count ourselves wise!

We are not wise—we are fools and blind, or we would cease from our self-glorifications and our scrambling after wealth, and we would save the perishing ones about us; we would make life better and sweeter for all, and try to live to the poet's ideal, and —

"Work for the good that is rightest,
Dream not of greatness afar ;
See that glory is ever the brightest,
Which shines upon men as thoy are."

Consumption is not transmitted from sire to son ; it is not inherited, it is not hereditary. It is not

born with a child any more than cholera or yellow
fever, or even toothache. We catch consumption as
we catch other infectious diseases, and if we devoted
one small tithe of the time and money to stamping
out consumption that we spend on ironclads and
implements of murder, we could soon stamp it out
But we wise Christian people, who have been busy
fighting for Gospel truths for nineteen hundred years,
are yet a long way from that eternal truth which will
make earth into heaven.

Consumption is caused by a tiny, rod-like worm,
which plays on the vital tissues, which lives on the
tender, succulent food stuff of the lungs, or in the
throat, or wherever else it can find a lodgment. Dr.
Koch, the great German, investigated the subject
thorough y, and showed just what the disease was
He took a colony of the tiny parasites from a tubercle
in a diseased human lung, and he transferred them to
prepared artificial food. He watched them reproduce
of their kind, in response to the law of merciless old
Dame Nature, who is as kind to the germs of a
deadly disease as she is to the sheep on a waterless
plain, as she is to the tenderest soul that ever
breathed a prayer. The scientific man removed a
new generation of germs to fresh food ; then, when
they had produced a new colony, he founded a fresh
colony, and so on for ten generations. Then he took
some of the artificially-raised germs, ten generations
distant from a diseased lung, and he inoculated living
animals, guinea pigs and other helpless forms, and lo !
they died of consumption. This is the working of
the mysterious power which falters never—

> "It slayeth and it saveth. nowise moved
> Except to the working out of doom ;
> Its threads are love and life, and death and pain
> The shuttles of its loom."

The red worm is consumption. The bright eye,
the hectic cheek, the gasping breath, the failing life,
these are the outward and visible signs of the
destruction of vital tissues by the red worm. When

a man comes of weak parents, who were cursed with delicate tissues, let him beware. When a man drinks and abuses his frame with excess, then he is undermining the constitution of the children yet unborn, for no man can suffer to himself alone. When a man with weak lungs catches cold, and the delicate lung stuff becomes abraded, he meets a gust of wind in George-street, or at Flemington market, and an organic "dust speck" finds a lodgment in his throat. It is a living speck, a dried, dessicated red worm, driven by the wind, seeking a spot to germinate, and it finds the required spot in the healthy lung that is abraded by a "bad cold," and in the course of a few months, or it may be years, the doctors declare that the man has consumption. It is a "visitation of Providence," perhaps, and at the funeral the minister says, "The Lord giveth and the Lord taketh away; blessed be the name of the Lord." We blame the Lord, or we blame the law, according to our mental bias, but we ought to blame the criminal folly of a gold-cursed, civilisation-maddened race. But Nature revenges herself on us by stealing our darlings, and bringing sorrow and gloom to once bright and happy homes—

> "She will not be contemned of anyone,
> Who thwarts her, loses, and who serves her gains;
> The hidden good she pays with peace and bliss,
> The hidden ill with pains."

When you visit the Thirlmere Home for consumptives—to which you ought to subscribe—you will find that every patient carries a box in his pocket, into which he must spit. No consumptive is allowed to expectorate about the house or the grounds, because there are cows and sheep and dogs about the place, and the red worms are in the sputen of the patients. The people about the Home know that if the patients were to spit about the place, the cattle would soon die; they know that such a "visitation" would not be the "visitation of God," but a deserved retribution for human carelessness. When a doctor suspects a patient of consumption, he has some of the saliva—the sputen—of the sick one collected, and he sends it to a bacteriologist or microscopist, who examines the matter under the keen eye of his powerful instrument. We sit round in the laboratory and wait for the verdict. When the scrutineer at last says, " Yes, here's the bacilli," we feel sorry, because, although we don't know the patient—we only know the doctor's name and the number on the bottle—we know that somebody has been sentenced to death, somebody's darling·—perhaps the only one—and we are sorry for the unknown victim. When people are under sentence of death from consumption, it takes great care and great sense to gain a reprieve. It's an awful disease.

We know the facts connected with it now. We know that consumptives are dangerous to all people with weak lungs or "bad colds," but because the disease is less forceful than cholera, less malignant than small-pox, and less sudden than diphtheria, we take no measures against it ; yet it is far more deadly than all these put together ! We allow consumptives to come to our shores from England ; we allow consumptives to walk our streets, and to expectorate in our trams, our offices and shops. The hot sun dries the sputen ; the wild southerly buster takes up the dessicated germs, and whirls them through all the city streets, into delicate lungs and sensitive throats, and more than 3,000 die in our fair land every year because of our blind, criminal, maudlin folly. We will not dare to look the matter in the face, and so we perish, and blame God for our sufferings. Fools that we are !

As with human beings, so with cattle. A correspondent has been enquiring if the disease is infectious or contagious. This is the answer. Here is the story. A healthy man or a healthy beast might eat the germs of consumption every hour of the day, and come to no harm, but when the weak one comes, or the weak hour, then comes the stealthy disease which plays such havoc with men and beasts. Tubercolosis in man is the same as in cattle, and we will never stamp out the disease in our beasts till we have stamped it out in human beings; but we ought to exercise great care over our dumb beasts, and kill them the moment we are certain they have tuberculosis. But what man or men will have the courage to take up this awful question? The sinful rulers who permit 3,000 human beings to die from consumption every year in Australia shriek fearsomely at the graziers and squatters who permit consumption in theit herds, but—who will take up the sword against our rulers, against this awful disease? Nature would not curse us, cursed we not ovrselves. We are the arbiters of our own destiny, for we can all believe that that force which rules the world is not a malevolent one, and most of us believe, with a great and wise one, that—

> "Before beginning, and without our end,
>   As space eternal and as surety sure,
> Is fixed a Power divine which moves to good,
>   Only its laws endure."

Fortune Telling.

WHEN Major Mitchell was exploring the Wellington Caves in 1838 he found some curious bones. He had never seen the like of them in his life, and he was clever enough to know that they were strangers to Australia. He shipped them off to Professor Owen, the great student of paleontology, and the results were peculiar. The great scholar took one big jawbone and studied it carefully, so that he could make out what other bones were required to fix it up into a perfect animal. When he had finished he had built up a beast— theoretically—such as no mortal man had ever seen on earth. It was not an elephant, nor a kangaroo, nor a rhinocerous, but it was like them all. It was a beast about nine feet long, seven feet high, that lived on vegetable stuff, and brought forth its young as a kangaroo does. It was a giant marsupialian, and he called it "Diprotodon Australis." Unbelievers laughed, because it was new to them, and impossible-looking, but the old man knew his scientific deductions were correct.

Watch a clever sheepbreeder at a pen, and he will pick out the kind of sheep he wants, and pay big prices for them, while an amateur fails to see where the value is. Every man to his business. The scientific man will tell you the history of a beast if you show him a section of its tooth. The scientific breeder will tell you the history of a beast by looking at its mouth.

Years passed away after Mitchell's discovery, and other men found other bones buried in the earth or hidden in caves, until we had all the bones of the "Diprotodon" gathered together, and built them up into the very shape that Professor Owen had sketched from a single bone. That is science! I had the pleasure of measuring the skeleton of one of these monsters myself in the Sydney Museum   There was no mistake about it.   Now we know that once, in the history of Australia, long before rain fairs were invented, or "labour members," or "unemployed," that there were vast multitudes of these monsters living in our country. We *know* that. It is not a surmise, or a guess, or a perhaps. It was so!

Professor Owen worked out his theories on a simple, scientific basis, called the law of homologous growth, and that is a law that we work on every day, but we don't know it. Go into a store in the back blocks and watch a station hand buying a pair of trousers He doesn't know how long his own leg is, in inches, but he takes hold of the trousers by the bottoms and stretches them out across his breast, with his arms extended. If he can just stretch the trousers out at full length, they will fit him. Why? Because he is built on the same plan as the "Diprotodon," and his arms and legs are in certain definite relationships to each other.

A New Zealand sheepbreeder ran out of collars the other day, and went into a Sydney store to buy some. The assistant said—

"What size do you wear?"

"I don't know."

The assistant took up a piece of twine that lay on the counter, and measured the New Zealander's *wrist*, not his neck. Then he doubled the string and said, "Twice round the wrist is once round the neck; that is the size you want, sir." And it was! The New Zealander and the "Diprotodon" were built on the same lines. The Apostle Paul said that "God hath made of one blood all nations of men to dwell together upon all the face of the earth." We know to day that God hath made of one blood, and on one plan, all the livings things that creep and crawl and fly and cheat and love and laugh and live on this old mud-ball of ours. We are made on the same plan as

the jackass and the kookaburra, the longwool sheep
and the merino ; we are brethren all, though some of
us despise our poor relations. You can tell the size
of a woman's foot by the size of her hand ; and you
can measure every organ of her body by some other
organ. If a woman is knitting a pair of stockings
for her husband, she never asks him to try them on
when she comes to the "narrowings"—not a bit of
it. She makes him shut his fist, and she wraps the
foot of the stocking round that to get the measure of
his pedal extremity. That is because her husband
is related to a " Diprotodon." We work on exactly
the same rule as Professor Owen, but we don't know
it.

Now, what has all this got to do with "fortune
telling?" It has everything to do with it ! If you
will look round Sydney now you will find that we are
swarming with "palmists," "fortune tellers," "astrologers," "necromancers," and all manner of people,
who dip into the future for you for a shilling, a half-
crown, or as much more as they can get. New
Zealand has been raiding them and punishing them,
and so will we after a while   But the question arises,
"Are they all frauds?" Not a bit of it ! Fortune
telling is pure, unmitigated humbug ! Fortune
telling is a fraud—a downright, unmitigated fraud,
but – character reading is possible, on Professor
Owen's basis, because—we are all relatives of the
" Diprotodon." If you can tell what a man is, you
can tell what he will do, and what he is likely to do.
There are men in the stock trade in Sydney that I
would go to if I was hard up and ask for their
assistance, and be sure of getting it, and getting it
with no grudging hand. There are other men, good
men in their way, that I would sooner die than ask a
favour from. You can tell by a man's face what he
is ; and how ? The best men are not the handsomest,
though I believe that good people are good-looking.
But there is something in a man's looks, or in his air,
that tells you what he is, and no man is good or bad

by accident ; he is what he is, because he was born
so ; and he is what he is, because of something he
had nothing to do with. George Eliot says—

"Our deeds still travel with us from afar,
And what we have been makes us what we are."

What our fathers and mothers were makes us what
we are, and what our unknown, remote ancestors
were makes us what we are also. A man is a queer,
animated sack of emotions, a child of accidents, and
occult incidents, such as should make us very tendei
in our judgments concerning our neighbours. Now,
if you can read a man's character from his face, or
his manner, or his general make-up, then you can tell
what he is likely to do in the future, and what he
has probably been able to do in the past. In addition to that, there is also that awful, cruel, merciless
law, which is written in letters of fire across the
earth's history—"Whatsoever a man soweth, that
shall he also reap," which is widened, deepened and
embittered by that other fearsome statement, that
"The sins of the fathers are visited upon the children,
even unto the third and fourth generation." You
may fool a parson, or a lawyer, but you can't fool
Nature ; you may even fool your wife, but the .aws
of the universe will not be trifled with. Behind all
these things lies the big delusion known as " Fortune
Telling."

CHAPTER II.

This is the best and loveliest world that any of
us ever saw, and, if all tales are true, it is the best
that any of us ever will see ; but, for all that, most
of us go through the world blind to its beauty. We
are like the sinners of old, who had eyes, but saw not,
and ears, but heard not. Some of us have our eyes
full of fat stock, and some are deafened by the clink
of golden counters—

" An idle poet here and there,
    Looks round him, but for all the rest,
    The world, unfathomably fair,
    Is duller than a witling's jest."

Some of us catch a glimpse of glory once in a
while, or hear the moving of mysterious things, but,
taking us for all in all, we are a stolid and stupid
race, marching on from the cradle to the grave with
no care for the lovely or glorious things about us.

At the recent ram fair we had men visiting us from
many far places, and they were but buyers or sellers,
mere items in the ledger—so many sheep, so many men,
so many sovereigns.   But we stood close to them for a
few days, and were startled to find that they were
human beings, with hearts and homes, and hopes and
fears, and aches and pains, just like ourselves.   One
of these men went with a well-known Sydneyite to a
palmist's and had his " fortune " told, and the palmist
read wonderful things from out his hand.   If I dared
to write the names of the two men, it would startle
my readers, but I may not name them ; let it suffice
to say that they were real men, and well-known men
in the circles of those interested in stock.   Is there
anything in fortune telling ?   Yea, verily there is !

Whenever a delusion or an idea has prevailed
throughout all the world for thousands and thousands
of years, there is something of truth in it, something
of real worth.   No great delusion that is all a
delusion can endure for long.   The salt of truth
must be there if the error is to be preserved.   Shakespeare says that we

    " Find tongues in trees, books in running brooks,
    Sermons in stones, and good in everything."

We, who are not Shakespeares, are too apt to
condemn what we cannot understand.   Now, let me
repeat a remark.   Fortune telling is pure, unmitigated humbug !   And let me add, also, that fortune
telling from character is true !   We meet men every
day who have scarcely got character enough to go to
the devil, and we meet men every day who are strong,

masterful and imperious. We can read their characters, though we don't know how. We all believe that a woman has keen intuitions; but so have children and dogs, and of him whom dogs and children dislike, do thou beware! Trust a woman, a dog, and a child!

How long has fortune telling endured? How long has the world endured? How long have men suffered, groaned, hoped and aspired? So long has fortune telling endured! Get that Bible out of your book-case, my worthy stock agent, and look up the 40th chapter of Genesis, and you will find there a yarn about a respectable fortune teller that will make you take off your hat to the profession of the palmist. A young man named Joseph was in quod, and amongst his fellow-prisoners were the king's butler and the king's baker. They each had a dream, and Joseph read their dreams for them—he told their fortunes! To the butler Joseph said: " In three days shall Pharaoh lift up thine head and restore thee unto thy place, and thou shalt deliver Pharaoh's cup into his hand after the former manner when thou wast his butler. But think on me when it shall be well with thee, and show kindness, I pray thee, unto me, and make mention of me unto Pharaoh, and bring me out of this house." Joseph was no fool, whatever Potiphar's wife might have thought!

When it came to the baker's turn to get his dream read, Joseph told him that " Within three days shall Pharaoh lift up thine head from off thee, and shall hang thee on a tree, and the birds shall eat thy flesh from off thee." And it came to pass just as the virtuous fortune teller had said. You know the rest! Pharaoh himself had a dream, and Joseph was brought out and read it, and became the boss of all Egypt—and there were no flies on him in that day! Do you wonder at the flock-master going to a Sydney arcade to get his fortune told after that? There's a good deal in fortune telling, and, if properly done, it can be relied on every time. Joseph was a good judge, and it's no use anybody setting up for a fortune teller unless they are good at reading character and talking double. That is, they must be able to talk as mysteriously as the Delphic Oracle, so that, whatever comes to pass, they may be right.

But how can you read a character from the hand? A man is built on scientific lines, for the Builder of the universe is scientific. A fellow student of mine, a devout young mathematician, when he saw the wonderful frost crystals on the window in a winter's morning, used to gasp out, in tones of deepest admiration, " God is a wonderful mathematician." He who trusts in God, and in God's ways, will never err. All men are built on one plan, and every characteristic of the individual is told in every part of his body. Some make a study of heads, and, by phrenology, read character; some study faces, and, by physiognomy, come to understand the nature of the being. The ears have recently been the subject of much study, and it will startle the densest sceptic to see how much character there is in ears. In Moslem countries the people take off their shoes where we take off our hats, and they leave them at the door of the Mosque, or the house, and they make a strange study. You can look at the row of shoes and slippers at the door of a Turkish mosque and read the character of the wearers. There is character in shoes, in gloves, in hair, in handwriting, in voices, and in a knock at the door.

Ask a wife if she knows her husband's step in the street. Ask a girl if she knows her sweetheart's knock at the door. Ask an auctioneer if he knows his buyers in a crowd. The Chinese don't photograph their criminals—they make them leave the impress of their thumbs on a sheet of rice-paper, and that can never be mistaken for anybody else's signature. Try it some night in your pleasant drawing-room. Get everybody to leave the imprint of the ball of the thumb on a sheet of white paper, and see how widely they differ. Character is written all over us, and you can tell what a man is likely to be by what he is and what he thinks, and "Whatsoever a man soweth, that shall he also reap."

A man is as he thinks. The central thought of the Cartesian philosophy is *cogito ergo sum*, or, in English, I think, therefore, I am, or, as we liberally render it, I am what I think. You watch a larrikin swinging along George-street with his "donah," and you will see his thoughts expressed in his walk. What a man thinks is expressed in his hand-shake, because what he is is written in his hand. Study the hands of the men about you, and you will soon see that every hand is different, unmistakably different, and the character is written in it, and he who studies hands can read characters, and he who can read characters can tell "fortunes." We never expect to gather figs from thistles, nor do we expect bad men to do good things, nor small-souled men to do great things. The character reader who can put two and two together can tell "fortunes" from hands, on a purely scientific basis, but no mortal man can lift the curtain of the morrow and tell aught save what might be. If any man declare aught else, he is a liar, and the truth is not in him.

CHAPTER III.

Blessed is the man who can laugh with the children, and remember not the years that weigh upon his head. Happy is he who can sing often—

" Turn back, oh, turn back, old Time, in your flight,
And make me a child again just for to-night."

If a man can shut his eyes to the mean things of life, and look only upon its pleasant side, then blessed is he indeed. The child that watches the transformation scene at the pantomime, and dreams not of the pulleys and dirt and grit behind the scenes, is happier than the man who knows how the "wheels go round." It is a bad thing to lose sight of the poetry of life, but when one sees the fraud and trickery practised by "fortune tellers" it makes the blood boil, for fools are always being swindled by it. Here is how it is worked, and it may be taken as a fair sample of how it can be done.

When I was younger than I am now (please excuse the autobiographical excursion), I landed in a large English city, and was invited by a friend to join a Good Templars' picnic. [P.S. — Nearly all journalists are Good Templars.] All the picnickers were strangers to me except one. There was a very pretty, giggly flirt in the crowd, whose name was Fannie. A party of young fellows seemed anxious to win her smiles, and she was no way shy. The man who was most in earnest was a dark-faced young fellow, whom his mates called "Billy," and on him Fannie smiled pleasantly, for he had a pretty good social position in the crowd. While we were awaiting tea in a large garden, I took to "fortune telling" to pass away the time, with the distinct understanding that it was all humbug. The fair flirt Fannie fooled round for a while, and I read her hand. It was easy to see that she had smiled on many men in her day, and she blushed about the "dark man" and the "fair man," for she had flirted with all sorts. But her heart was pining for a real lover, and I "saw one in her hand," and described Billy, who was rather peculiar in his ways. She was to marry the "dark man," and have several children, and a good deal of trouble, etc., etc.

Then Billy came along and presented his horny paw. He had never had a real, true love till now, and he had been born to hard work. He was going to marry a "fair girl," and here followed an accurate description of Fannie. Knowing that I was a stranger, and could not possibly be acquainted with them, they took it in good part, and, with the distinct understanding that it was all humbug, we parted. About a year afterwards I gave a lecture on the frauds connected with "fortune telling," explaining the little truth that lay at the bottom of it, but cursing the impostures that it gave rise to. At the close of the lecture a very pretty girl came to me and said, " There's a great deal of truth in fortune telling, in spite of what you say, because you told my fortune once, and it came true in every particular nearly," and she giggled until I recognised the Fannie of the picnic. A year or two later I met Fannie out with a perambulator, and the " dark man," Billy, close beside her. They had made their own fortunes, and thought it had all been written in their hands by the good God who made the universe. That couple believe implicitly in fortune telling, because—oh, because the " Globe Trotter" read their hands, and he didn't know a thing about them ; but he told them "all sorts of things that happened in the past, and just who they were going to marry—and it all came true." Exactly so—poor fools that they were ! Anybody can tell fortunes on that basis ! So do "fortune tellers" often astonish simple people, who really declare their own lives to the keen eyes of the professional " palmist."

But, besides all this humbug, there are certain lines in the hand that denote certain characteristics. A sheepbreeder can run his eyes over a sheep and tell you its chief point of merit or demerit. He may not be able to put into exact words the reason for the faith that is within him, but he knows what constitutes the chief points in an animal. We all know a good deal more than we can tell, and most of us believe a good deal more than we know, but one thing is certain in us all—we see a good many things that we are incapable of explaining. Look at your own hand, and study the lines on it. In the average hand there is a line runs along the base of the fingers, say an inch down the palm. That is called, in the art of the palmist, the line of the heart. If it is very wide at the part nearest the little finger, it denotes a vivid imagination ; if it is abnormally wide it denotes a weak intellect. You can only arrive at an idea of what is normal by studying a lot of hands. Now, trace that line over towards the index finger. If it runs straight across it denotes an equable temperament, and tells that the owner is easy to get along with ; if it turns up abruptly between the index and the next finger, it means self-will, which may easily run into pig-headedness. It is here that a man's obstinacy, self-will, or real grit is notified. If the line divides, and one part runs up and the other runs down between the fingers, it indicates, as a rule, self-will, along with easiness to lead. It means a way of your own, along with the grace of yielding.

A little lower down is another line, crossing the palm, running, to some extent, parallel to the other. That is called the line of the head. It begins between the index finger and the thumb If it ends before reaching the centre of the palm, it indicates a poor intellectual capacity ; if it crosses the centre of the palm it indicates a good capacity ; if it runs over to the edge of the hand, it tells of the power for retaining money ; if it divides at the edge of the palm, it indicates a lack of what we term honesty. Some New Zealanders have that bifurcation, and that is why they sold some wethers for rams. They couldn't help doing that, because the line divided. We are what we are, because we were born so, though Goethe says, "Some of our weaknesses are born in us, others are the result of education ; it is a question which of the two give us the most trouble."

Another line, running round the base of the thumb, is called the line of life. It begins, also between the forefinger and thumb. If it is clean cut, deep and continuous down to the wrist, it denotes descent from a line of strong, healthy people. Years ago a young Hercules was visiting me, a strong, well-built, splendid fellow. I looked at his hand and said, laughingly, "Why, Sam, you're going to die young." That was said because he looked so strong, and because I had not then come to realise the truth that lies hidden in the hand. He said, "Yes, I know that. My father dropped dead when he was thirty-five. It is the heart that troubles my family." The deep pathos in his voice gave me the horrors, and I rarely read hands now, and *never* tell all I see.

These are the main lines of the truth that underlie the fortune teller's miserable trade, and these form the basis of all the delusions that have made the business so enduring through all the ages of the world. Why those lines denote certain things I know not, *but they do*. Because they do, the fortune teller flourishes, and all human beings desire, at some time or other, to lift the curtain of the morrow, and the Quaker poet only voiced the mighty yearning when he sang—

" Oh, Thou, our morrow's pathway knowing,
Through the strange world round us growing,
Speak and tell us where we're going."

CHAPTER IV.

The editor of this paper said, "We don't want any more articles on "Fortune Telling," Mr. 'Globe Trotter,'" but an advertisement in last Saturday's *Herald* made him re-consider that order. It was a lovely advertisement, that might have been been paid for by the "Globe Trotter" just to show how true his words were. It was inserted by "M. Jaffar Najjar, Egyptian geological and astrological diviner." That was in the *S.M. Herald* of Saturday, July 21, 1894. Joseph and Mrs. Potiphar and Pharaoh and that crowd are not so very far away, after all. And all the fools are not dead yet. Some hard-headed stock agents would have you believe that fortune telling is old and played out, and musty-fusty foolish, but it is all alive and kicking, as our dear brother, M. Jaffar Najjar, could probably testify.

He tells fortunes by means of the earth and the

stars. He will read your fortune from a sand-heap, as I have seen the Arabs do in a Moslem market-place. He will tell your fortune from the earth by geological methods, or from the stars, if you will pay to have your horoscope cast. Let me tell you a story, sweet and sympathetic readers. Once upon a time, and a middling—very middling—good time it was, a very long time ago, I was teaching a Sunday-school class in a little village, inhabited chiefly by darkies, the most of whom were runaway slaves from the Southern States. They were a simple and child-like lot, and they looked upon me as a very wise man, so that showed that they were very ignorant. One Sunday afternoon I was explaining to them that we live on a globe, and we are circling round the sun, upheld by a power which passeth all understanding. At noon we are on top, nearest the sun, and at mid-night we are underneath, furthest away from the sun. Of course, we all believe that, or we think we do, or we don't think about it at all ; but we would probably say we believed it if we were asked. The darkies took in that yarn without a word, and I thought it was all right, but if Brother Jaffar had been at the door of the school-room when we came out he would have laughed.

My class was waiting for me outside, and the village blacksmith, Jim Baker, was the spokesman. He looked at me very solemnly, and said, . " Look'e heah, massa ! Don' you say we's a-livin' on a globe ? " making a sphere with his hand as I had done. " Yes." " An' don' you say as we'se up heah at dinner time, and we's down heah at night ? " motion-ing with his hands. " Yes " " Well, look'e heah, how is it we don't tumble off when we'se down heah, eh ? " and Jim roared with laughter at my silly conceit, and all the assembled darkies joined in right scornfully. There was a mean nigger named Ben, who used to peddle watermelons, stood at the back of the crowd, and when the first laugh had subsided he said, " How is it all de water don' run out ob de wells when de wells is upside down, eh ? Yah, yah, ha!" and he yelled at his own idea.

From that day forth my influence over the darkies had gone. They wrote me down an ass. Any man who held such a fool theory as that was unfit to boss a nigger meeting, and they scorned me ; but they would have believed in Brother Jaffar. They believed that this old world of ours was the centre of the universe, and that the sun, moon and stars were but the adjuncts thereto, set to give us light, or to beautify the sky about us. Not only did they believe this, but they believed that anybody who did not share their belief was a fool, if not a knave. They would have fought like tigers for their belief, too, because they were like the men of old, of whom it was said they—

> " Prove their doctrines orthodox,
> By Apostolic blows and knocks ;
> Call fire and sword and desolation
> A godly, thorough reformation."

One of the most egotistical and magnificent impertinences on earth is the one that weaves the destiny of the man in with that of the star The idea that the meanest loafer on the Domain affects the remotest star, and that the movements of the most kingly star in the heavens is interwoven with the fate of the meanest Domain loafer, is simply sublime impudence. Yet that is what astrology means. Nobody but an ignoramus could assume for a moment that the stars could tell him a cure for liver worm in his sheep, yet Brother Jaffar probably would. No man with the least claim to physical knowledge would think of consulting the stars about the state of his wife's health, or the winner of the Melbourne Cup ; yet that is the kind of folly that crowds the Sydney papers to-day with the advertisement of seers, palmists, astrologers and quacks. And it has been so for many a weary century, for Hudibras tells the same things of the Brother Jaffars of two centuries ago, who—

'' Feed the pulses of the stars
To find out agues, coughs, catarrhs ;
And tell what crisis does divine
The rot in sheep, or mange in swine.''

But what think ye of a few facts like these?
The earth—this great, big, fevered, bustling world of
ours—is, say, 25,000 miles in circumference. It
circles round the sun in 365 days, at the rate of
68,000 miles an hour. You need to say a thing like
that slowly, so you can take it in. The Western
train goes tearing along from Sydney at the rate of
30 miles an hour sometimes ; and if, when it was
going at that rate, it ran into another train, or on to
a rock, it would make a fearful smash up. Well,
this world where we were born, and where we worry,
and where we bury, is travelling at the rate of
68,000 miles an hour, and never stops for wood, or
water, or Sundays, or elections, or anything else.
The sun, round which it revolves, is 92 million miles
away. You couldn't send frozen mutton there, eh?
What about your 12 or 14 thousand miles to Europe
now? That sun is close to us compared to the stars.
The nearest star is so many millions and billions of
miles distant that the mention of it only reveals how
much a man doesn't know. If you were to travel 92
million miles to the sun, and have a " smoke-oh " and
look round, you wouldn't be an inch nearer to the
stars. They are so far away that 92 million miles
don't make any difference to them. Oh, Brother
Jaffar !

The fixed stars are suns, some of them bigger
than our sun, and our great, big, fiery sun, that
sucks up all the water on the plains and drinks up
all our rivers, and robs our flocks of water, and
brings death to sheep and sundowners, is only a baby
star itself. Our sun is only a speck in the universe,
a sand grain amid the multitude of stars that fleck
the shoreless sea of the infinite. And our earth?
Poor little wandering speck of fire-spun matter. If
our sun is a speck, then what is our earth? Poor,

pitiful little speck, circling round a larger speck!
The suns endure for millions of years, but a man is
old at three score years and ten, and he lays him
down and sleeps, and his mental parts are rendered
up to the elements, and he who was once a king
becomes but a mass of undistinguishable phosphates,
while the mighty stars still burn and shine. And
Brother Jaffar will read the stars and tell you how
it will prosper with the wool you sent to Europe;
how it will fare with your love, and your business,
your pleasure and your woe. He will tell you—for the
stars know it all—when you will die, and, perhaps,
where you will go to after that. Ha! ha! This is
a mad world, my masters, a mad world indeed!

But listen! We, in our sublime ignorance,
hitch the passionless, sky-travelling, space-despising
orbs of heaven to our little hives, and dream
not of impertinence; but what about the Jaffars!
The advertisement in the *Herald* will explain that.
Brother Jaffar says that he wrote to the *Herald* in
February, 1894, to inform the electors that at the
" general election the policy of the Government would
be ' Protection.' " He meant by that that the election
would result in the return of Protectionists, and he
says, " ' Lord, who hath believed our report?' "
That's just what I would say, indeed! But he
proceeds to say that he is quite firm in his prediction,
and that he has done this " to demonstrate to atheists,
agnostics and materialists that only the Deity rules
the universe, and, in His providence, endows with
this power whosoever He will, as you will find hereafter." Good, Jaffar! He foretold what would
happen, and it didn't happen, and now he advertises
in the daily papers to show that he meant it, and you
had better look out; and that is just like a fortune
teller. Astrologers have a bad time of it generally
in an unbelieving place like Sydney, but if Jaffar
could give us a tip for the Melbourne Cup he need
never do another stroke of work in his life. The
stars can tell you a lot of things, but never a thing

that is of the slightest use. Poor stars! Happy, happy Jaffar ! Astrology is dead, except for fools ! Palmistry is kept alive by the cuteness of its adepts ; cards and teacups are almost discredited, but they still linger with us in odd .corners.   But when we read an advertisement like Jaffar's, we realise, in a dim way, something of the world's undying folly and we—

> " Look up to the great wide sky,
>   Enquiring wherefore we were born
>   For earnest or for jest."

Money-Lenders' Tricks.

GOOD many years ago I knew a religious man, a very religious man, who took up the business of lending money. He had seen advertisements of "Christian men" who had money to lend to widows and orphans, and it seemed to him to be a good business. He wanted to help the widow and the orphan on "reasonable terms," and serve God while he worshipped mammon. He scooped in his fellow Christians until he had secured a regular nest of deacons, elders and parsons to form the company, and the way it was done was pitiful.

A good man strolled into the office one day, and the religious man invited him to join the money-lending business. The good man flared up and said, "No; I like to know what my money is doing. I don't want to be making my interest out of the blood of miserable failures." He was a good man. When the religious man got to talking about 25 per cent., and perhaps more, it undermined the good man's resolutions, and he finally took a large number of shares. Poor man! When the devil comes in plausible shape, offering a large return, it s hard to resist him, especially when a church deacon holds the bait. It's very easy for some of us moneyless ones to criticise our neighbours, but Burns put the matter well when he said—

> " Then at the balance let's be just,
>   We never can adjust it ;
> What's done we partly may compute,
>   But know not what's resisted."

It was something of a comfort to see that loan society go " bung," and all the religious men left regretting their softness, while the good men were repenting of their folly.   But the discovery the religious money-lenders made was a curious one. They found that there were a lot of reckless, adventurous, good-for-nothing wretches in the world, whose sole means of livelihood appeared to be that of preying on money-lenders.   If a man with a soul goes into the usury business, he will have to sell his soul at an early date, or go bung.   A sympathetic money-lender, a money-lender with bowels of compassion, is of no account.   He must be dead to all the tender feelings of humanity, and be able to sing, with Rudyard Kipling—

" We have done with Hope and Honour, we are lost to Love
      and Truth ;
We are dropping down the ladder rung by rung."

We can pity a money-lender for what he once was, but beware of him to-day.   Here is how the thing works :   A selector, who lives not more than 2,000 miles from Sydney, was hard pushed for cash— as we all are just now – and he saw the advertisement of a money-lender.   It was such a nice little advertisement.   You would think that the man who inserted it had corns on his hands with giving out money to poor people.   You would think the man who put that advertisement in was a real Christian with a heart as big as all out of doors, and a sympathy as wide as the world.   This man who lent money— we'll call him Jones, because that's not his name — said he never refused an applicant, and he charged no fees ;   and he was one of the kindest, nicest men in the world.   It was an advertisement that was brimming over with the song—

" Will you walk into my parlour ? "

This selector, whom we will call Smith, because his name isn't Smith, applied for a loan, and he knows now how some loan offices are worked.   He has "been there," so to speak, and he knows. He received a real nice, cordial, friendly reply, written by the same hand as wrote the advertisement. It said there would be no trouble about a loan at all, and they would attend to it at once ! That was nice. It filled his soul with hope, and he saw himself walking into the village grocery to pay his long-standing account. He revelled in the joy of having a balance at the bank once more, and he had a good time over it. Then Mr. Jones wrote to say that they would need to send a valuator on behalf of their client who was advancing the money, because, of course, it wasn't Jones and Co. who were advancing the money Oh, no ! They were simply the agents, as it were. Their hearts were tender and sympa-thetic, and things—and they were only acting for others. It didn't say so in the advertisement, but, then, that was a detail. However, it was only fair that the selection should be valued, even if it were going to cost £12 12s. cash, in advance ; so Smith borrowed that from a friend. The valuator came out and had a look round. He was a nice man, and seemed so pleased with the place. He was a real good man for his business, for he made Smith feel that he had a lovely place, and that he was doing the right thing in borrowing money of Jones. He was a nice man !

Then there was a delay of a few days, and Smith kept watching for a letter, and going into town every post and bailing up every passer-by who might have brought the letter with a cheque in it, but—it didn't come. When a letter came at last it had no cheque in it. Mr. Jones found that his client " would require a plan of the selection, and we could scarcely object to that ; but we regret that it will cost £3 3s. at the Lands Office. If you send that sum along we will have a tracing made at once, and you can come down and sign the deeds, and all will be well." Mr. Jones was so sorry for giving all the trouble, but—"if you remit the £3 3s. you can come down on Thursday next and complete the transaction."

Poor Smith! His whole heart was fixed on the idea of getting the money. Ho borrowed from his agents the three guineas, and the fare and expenses to Sydney. He sent the money along, then he came to town with a wildly-beating pulse. At the appointed time he went to look for the gorgeous office of the great financier Jones, who used such stylish note-paper, and he was startled at what he discovered. The office was up such a lot of stairs! There was no furniture in it, except a stool, an old chair, a ricketty table, and a waste-paper basket! Jones was evidently a philanthropist! He lived with the simplicity of a Stoic, and, by virtue of his self-denial, was able to help the suffering world. He was there himself, but his "client," for whom he acted, was not. He would be in to-morrow, and Smith would get a note at his hotel, telling him when to come round and get the money. Next morning a note came to say that "We deeply regret to inform you that our client refuses to make the advance upon your selection." That was all!

Poor Smith! It had cost him £20 to find out that Jones was a scheming, silver-tongued devil, who had no money and no intention of raising money for him. It had cost him over £20 to find out what his agents could have told him first off. It cost him over £20 to realise the depth of his own folly. It cost him over £20 to find out what some of us have known for many years. There are "money-lenders" in Sydney who never lend a shilling, but live on the "fees" of poor men like Smith. There are miserable ghouls in Sydney who live in clover when times are bad, and revel on the misfortunes of their fellows. They are the carrion crows of civilisation, and should be torn to pieces by wild horses; but what can be done? What could Smith do? He had no legal remedy. When he went back to the office he found that Jones was absent. He might, certainly, have kicked him to death if he had found him, but that was all he could do, and that wouldn't bring back his £20 Poor Smith !

If you must borrow money, Mr. Selector, write to your town agents, or somebody you know, and deal with a square firm, for there, probably, are "square firms," but borrowing money is a bad business. "He who goes a-borrowing goes a-sorrowing," and don't you forget it.

Maŋ-made Calendars,

F New South Wales had sense she would fall down and worship the Seventh-Day Adventists. They come like the Waverley pens, "as a boon and a blessing to men." These Adventists ought to set us all to thinking, and, if so, they would deserve canonisation, but they won't ! We are such a fat-headed lot of fools that even Adventists fail to reach our intellects. Some of us will write to the *Daily Telegraph*, and some of us will settle the matter by calling them fools, but very few of us will sit down to think the thing out.

You would imagine, to hear some people talk, that Seventh-Day Adventism was new, and that this trouble about which day is the "Lord's Day" was a modern affliction, but it isn't. Julius Cæsar tried to fix it up, but he couldn't. You ask Galton, the imported historian of New South Wales ! He doesn't know much about New South Wales, but he knows a good deal about Julius Cæsar ! He could, probably, tell you how J.C. tried to arrange the calendar, and did arrange it too, but it all tumbled to bits, and Pope Gregory had to fix it up again in another 1500 years or so. These Parramatta Adventists are stale, stale as ditch-water, but we don't know it.

When I was a boy they brought me up piously —anybody could tell that—and made me believe that the seventh day was the Sabbath, and that a man was put up into the moon for picking sticks on a Sunday—and Sunday, of course, was the seventh day ! We nearly all believed that once ! There are men in Sydney who put on a clean shirt and a nice suit of clothes on the first day of every week out of respect to that old fetish even now. But a sad awakening came to me.

When I was young and guileless I used to go trading across the Pacific from 'Frisco to China. When we crossed some particular spot in the Pacific Ocean we dropped a day, or gained a day, according to the direction we were going in. Coming from California we gained a day, and I always yearned to come to the jump on a Sunday, so that we would have two "duff days," two idle days, in one week; but we never did! We always got to the jump on a pork day! That was the cheapest day for the owners. When we were going the other way we always lost a ".duff day." None of us understood it, but we caught on to the idea that the skipper had arranged it somehow; so he did! The calendar is a matter of simple business calculation, and if men weren't fools they would see it, and would never talk about stocks for Adventists. Perhaps the subject is too deep for men who deal in frozen meat and sheep and cattle and horses and station stuff? Not a bit of it; they are not the men who cry—

" Ever the problem besets me, in labour, in sorrow, in laughter;
Mystery of mysteries, too wide for conception, too deep and too high!
Imbecile! What doth it profit to gaze on the mists of Hereafter?
Turn me away from them. Eat, drink, be merry; to-morrow we die."

The readers of the *Stock Journal* are men of sense, and the question of the calendar is not a religious one, but a business one. The sap-heads of Adventists and their silly opponents are making it a religious question, but they are—clams!

When the world was flat, and the entire earth was under the flap of the Roman Eagle's wing, it was easy for the king to say, " Let the day after to-morrow be a day of rest." But when Copernicus came along and said the world was round, it was awkward. When Copernicus said that the sun was not made to rule the day, but that our mud-ball circled round the sun, it was worse. It took the starch out of some of the mighty ones. It began to look as if our earth were only "small potatoes, and few in a heap," and if Copernicus hadn't died about the time he did, there would have been grave trouble for him.

When the little, lame Portuguese navigator, Ferdinand Magellan, started out on his wonderful voyage round the world, and came out into our Pacific Ocean, through the straits that bear his death-less name, he discovered strange things. He saw the Southern Cross ; he saw the white clouds that we call to-day "Magellan's Clouds." He saw strange islands and strange races, such as Christian men had never seen before. He hungered, thirsted, suffered and enjoyed as few men have ever done ; but the miserable, small-souled wretches who voyaged with him murdered him somehow, or somewhere, nobody knows how, poor little soul ! He never lived to discover that calendars were made by men, and not by gods.

When Magellan's ships returned, after three years' absence, by way of the Cape of Good Hope, and reached civilisation, they discovered a horrible thing. They were a day out in their reckoning ! They had been keeping saints' days, holy days, feast days, fast days, and Sundays on the wrong day, for— heaven knows how long. Yet the Lord was not angry with them. The Lord of heaven and earth is kinder to us than our fellow creatures.

What is it that Faber says ? Something like this—

"There's a wideness in God's goodness,
 Like the wideness of the sea ;
There's a kindness in his justice
 That is more than liberty."

Magellan's sailors discovered that Sunday is a geographical arrangement, and that feast days and holy days are arranged, not by high Heaven, but by earthly calendar makers !

When the early men first began to measure time,

they had an awful problem to solve. You see, if the king were born in the Grecian month of Mary—only Mary's month hadn't been invented then – they celebrated it in the sweet summer time; but every year the birthday got further and further away from the summer time, until, when the king was old and feeble, his birthday came in mid-winter. It took the priests, and the soothsayers, and· the wise men hundreds of years to try and fix up a calendar that would bring the king's birthday or the saturnalia at the same season of the year. It was a good Pope (God rest him!) who fixed us up at last with $365\frac{1}{4}$ days in a year, and 366 in a leap year, to even things up. That was in 1582, but we good Protestants wouldn't accept anything of the kind. We protested against it, and refused to accept any " Popish innovations." We're a wise family ! But all the crowd that bucked against the Pope is dead—

> " Their bones are dust,
> And their swords are rust,
> And their souls are with the saints
> We trust."

The Catholics get along all right after the Pope arranged things, but the Protestant calendar kept getting worse and worse, until at last Lord Chesterfield brought in a bill, in the reign of George II., to drop eleven days and get even with the Catholics. If J. C. Neild had been along about that time, he'd have had a picnic ! In spite of the jawbones of that day, the bill was passed, and it was arranged that on September 3rd, 1752, the calendar should be shifted on to September 14th! What a howl it raised, and no wonder. Fancy, when the spooks came out to walk on All Souls' Eve, they would get mixed. The Catholic spirits would be on the wallaby track eleven days before the Protestant spirits, if they attended to the calendar made by Act of Parliament. And now the Parliament was going to fix it so that the same night would suit them both. All the Jawbone Neilds of the land rose up and yelled

"Give us back our eleven days." "Down with the Pope." "Who stole our eleven days?" but it was no use. We dropped eleven days, and still grew, like the Galatians, to reverence the new days and times and seasons, just as if God had arranged them. As a small boy I was taught that Sunday was the seventh day, which God had ordered to be kept holy, and when the skipper arranged the change on the Pacific Ocean, it was an awful shock to me, but why should it be so? Why can we not be as honest about our religion as about our daily business? Some of us give up work on one day of the week—all right enough, if we are not on the daily press—but if we had sense we would try to arrange it so that we would only work one day in the week and play the rest. Instead of accepting the calendar as a man-made institution, and making it a good day, here we go talking about putting up stocks for a silly Adventist who wants to obey the Scripture as he reads it, and keep some other day holy. Listen to me, dear readers. A man who wants to keep holy one day in the week is either a fool or a knave, or both. Good men ought to keep holy every day, and never try to keep one day holy to the hurt of the others. But a lot of us pray on our knees on a Sunday, and prey on our neighbours through the week, and of such is the kingdom of cant.

Hydatid Cysts.

DID you ever read "Three Men in a Boat?" Do you remember the one who read a doctor's book and found that one of the signs of liver disease was a disinclination to work? He had suffered from that disease all his life, and his cruel father had tried to cure him with a stick. That man read the doctor's book, and found in himself the signs of every disease referred to except "Housemaids' Knee." If you are given that way, don't read this article; put down the paper at once, or else turn to "Flotsam and Jetsam," or something light. But, reader, if you like to sup on horrors and revel in real ghastliness, just light your pipe, sit down, and let's have a yarn.

In our last issue there was a brief account of a little girl in Goulburn having a great big hydatid taken out of her skull. It must have been a fearful operation, but it shows what strides surgical science is making. We hope that by-and-bye the surgeons will be able to cut the bad parts out of a baby's brain and make an incipent scoundrel into a sweet and virtuous citizen.

In Iceland, that strange, cold, volcanic island in the North Atlantic, about one-sixth of the total death-rate is due to hydatids. Not because the place is cold exactly, but partly because the people are poor, and suffer from cold. It's this way. The Icelanders all keep dogs, and dogs keep hydatids. The men are fond of their dogs, and, as the climate is deadly cold, they have to keep them indoors in winter time, so the dogs often sleep in the same bed as the peasants. Then, too, they eat off the same plate, and, if the Icelander is not *very* particular, he allows the dog's lick to serve instead of a washing. Now, dogs are the nursing mothers of hydatids. Over 28 per cent. of Icelandic dogs are crawling with hydatids, so it is no wonder that the disease is very prevalent amongst the people.

What are hydatids? Why, tapeworms, of course! The word is from the Greek *hydatis*, a watery vesicle, and the grown-up, sexual, hydatid is a tape-worm that lives in a dog or a wolf. If you ask a scientific prig what a hydatid is, he may tell you that it is a *Tænia echinococcus*, and that its method of reproduction is peculiar, and that " the casting off of the sexual segments is in some respects comparable to the detachment of the hectocotylized arm of a cephalopod, and the formation of new joints to the development of an Oligochætous worm." Then you know all about it.

In Sydney we have a fearful lot of mangy, miserable, masterless dogs If they were killed and examined, a lot of them would be found to be full of tiny tape-worms, such as give rise to hydatids. When these tape-worms give birth to eggs, they are such small specks of things as to be invisible to the naked eye. These are extruded from the dog in different ways, but the chief way is by the mouth of the beast. They come upwards on to its tongue, and when the dog licks itself they cling to its hair. When it drinks they are set free in the water. They mingle with its excreta and haunt the kennel. They are everywhere. A little girl in New South Wales was very fond of the family dog—all little girls are— she cuddled it and kissed it and made it her playmate. After a while it was discovered that there was a strange growth in her inside. The doctors said she had hydatids. She was put under chloroform and opened, and the doctors took out a great mass of stuff from her inside, which they called a " hydatid cyst " The tiny worms from the long-forgotten dog had passed into her stomach The gastric juices had thawed them out, and a tiny, six-clawed worm had fastened on to her stomach and eaten its way out into the blood, and had settled in her abdomen. Then it lost its claws, and settled down to reproduce of its kind by budding. It built itself a case from out the tissues of the little girl's body, and on the inside of the case it budded and spread and increased until it weighed about seven pounds, and the little girl seemed to be dying. Then the doctors took out the mass and saved her life.

That is many a year since. She grew up to womanhood. She had a sweetheart, and was married to him, and life was very pleasant on the lovely hillside where they dwelt, until she became ill. They thought it was the natural state of young wives, but she grew ghastly-looking, and was dying while she walked and worked. Then the doctors came and diagnosed her case, and said it was hydatids. Another operation, and they removed from her an enormous cyst, weighing nearly twenty pounds! The tiny eggs from some favourite dog had wrought sore havoc with her. We met the poor, weak woman when on a vacation away from the roar of Sydney life, and it was pitiful to look upon her. How came the second attack? Had the cyst broken and allowed an escape, which developed into proper tape-worms? Had they lived all these years cursing the woman's life? Who shall say? Life is a mystery; we come from the earth, and we return to the earth, and thus many a strange chance happens to us on the road, but we know little more about it all than did Lucretius, the noble Roman, who died ere Christ was born. He sang, in that old long ago—

> "Then learn
> That what of us was taken from the dust
> Will surely one day to the dust return ;
> And what the air has lent us Heaven will bear
> Away and render back its own to air."

What a strange rendering up it is when the hydatid takes the process in hand.

The bladder worm, as it is often called, was

known to the great Aristotle, and to Hippocrates, but how it came to the birth none dared to say. For long ages it was believed to be the product of spontaneous generation, a free gift of the devil ; but in 1781 Pallas, the naturalist, suggested that it, maybe, came from an egg. Then, in 1845, the famous Steenstrup came out with the theory of the alternation of generation. That was a novel theory, but see how it worked in the liver-fluke. See how each generation was different from its predecessor, until we had worked a whole round of living things to get back to the old liver-fluke. So is it with this fearsome thing that is spreading so rapidly in Australia. The hydatid cyst taken from the little girl's skull at Goulburn was the child of the tape-worm that once lived in a dog. A great doctor, Kuchenmeister, collected a large number of cysts, and their history showed what a dreadful curse the disease is. A large number of cysts were taken from the brain, where they used to be always fatal. Sixteen cyst bearers showed no signs of disease during life ; in six there were slight signs of derangement ; twenty-four were cases of epilipsy, six of cramp, forty-two of paralysis, and twenty-three of mental disturbances of varying degrees of intensity. What a suggestion of epileptics and paralytics from this accursed disease, from the growth of this horrible cyst. The small worm, the first tiny visitor, gets into the currents of the blood, and may find a rest anywhere. It goes dancing through the veins in the red current of the life, and no man can tell where it will anchor. A great doctor went carefully into the subject to test some previous experiments, and of all the cases examined he found that 46 per cent. of the drifting worms had made a home in the liver, six per cent. in the brain, $3\frac{1}{2}$ per cent. in the heart. Some were in the lungs, some in the muscular tissues, and some even in the bones. He affirmed that 25 per cent. of the cases proved fatal.

How do you get hydatids ? By drinking impure

water, by eating salads that grow in damp places in Chinamen's gardens, by caressing dogs, by all the thousand and one processes of life. You cannot guard against the horrors, but now that the disease is spreading in Australia we ought to start a crusade against unclean dogs, and against pet dogs inside cosy houses. We should shriek out when we see children fondling dogs, and if we were wise we would scald the kennels of our favourites frequently. It is the most awful curse of modern life, for these hideous tapeworm born cysts reach to even 30 lbs. weight inside of a poor mortal, and the torture of them is past all description. Reader, fill pur pipe again, and take this horrible story to heart. Don't try and feel if you have any hydatids about you; but, for the sake of those who are suffering now, try and awaken attention to this dread disease, and prevent it from spreading further.

Spiritualistie Experiences.

CHAPTER I.

HE Methodists have one of the finest plans for spiritual development that ever was invented. One of the Wesleys put it in order for them. It is this : On a certain night of each week the members of the congregation are to meet with certain holy men, appointed leaders, in what is called a "class," and are there to relate their "experiences," and the "leader" will give them such words of reproof, advice, or consolation, as may be deemed necessary. If all the Methodists lived up to their "class-night" experiences, they would conquer the world, but, unfortunately, they cannot do it. They dare not speak out for themselves. They acquire a parrot-like form of expression, and if you attend a "class" for a few nights you will be able to tell what every member is going to say. That is because of the famous amount of sheepishness that exists in our race. All we like sheep go after our leader. But that is not purely a Methodist weakness. If you send a reporter to a place to look up a series of facts, you can measure him up and tell what he will see before he goes. Reporters are not Methodists, as a rule, but they *are* methodists in their way. A Sydney reporter is doing the spiritualistic business in Sydney just now, and he is making the most awful mess of it. His reports are just a little bit worse than anything that ever saw the light before in a professedly intelligent paper.

Before making any remarks on spiritualism, please allow me to explain. Any man who makes unkind remarks about his neighbour's religion is a

Philistine. We ought to respect a man's religion. But, as an old journalist, I claim a right to throw stones at the miserable professors of all classes. I've lived amongst religions of many kinds, and have a profound regard for some of them. I've gone to "make chin-chin for Joss" at a Chinese temple, and have slunk out of sight of the fiery Moslem zealots who were making martyrs of themselves to please Allah. I've seen all kinds of religions on tap, and respect them all, but I'm down on the shams who belong to them. Spiritualism is a religion to some people, so I haven't a word to say against it; but the editor of the "Stock and Station Journal" wants my views on the subject, my "experiences," as it were, so hats off, gentlemen!

A Boston editor said to me one time, "Do you know anything about spiritualism?"

"No, sir."

"Got any prejudices against it?"

"No, sir."

"All right. You're the man I want to investigate it."

A famous lady was in Boston at the time, Mrs. Beecher Hooker, a sister of Henry Ward Beecher and of Mrs. Beecher Stowe, of "Uncle Tom's Cabin." This Mrs. Beecher Hooker was a spiritualist, and she had with her a famous "medium" named Mrs. Maud Lord. I went to their public demonstration, admission one dollar—that's a part of the show that hurts, because there's always somebody to scoop the pool. When a man like Talmage comes along, purely on the make, of course you can't say a word against him; but when a man or a woman comes along with a brand new religion the dollar hurts. Being a pressman, I went in "on the nod," of course, but the dollar gave me a bad taste in my mouth all the same!

On the platform the woman with the strong Beecher face talked about spirits in a familiar way that startled a man like me, for I had been brought up to talk about the Holy Ghost in a reverent way;

but Mrs. Beecher Hooker didn't seem to see any holiness about ghosts at all   However, that is probably a matter of education and early training.   She introduced Maud Lord, a bouncing, black-eyed, lascivious-looking woman who could talk—whew ! She fooled that audience to the fullest extent, and told such infamous crammers that Baron Munchausen was a fool beside her.   But, then, it seemed to me that they had paid their dollars to get fooled, and they certainly got what they paid for.

I was introduced to her at the close, and she was gracious— very gracious, and invited me to a " dark seance," to take place at her house the following Wednesday night. I was there, like a little man, and walked in without paying my dollar, even though the "medium " did not recognise me, which I thought passing strange.   Her henchman was a Scotchman, who knew me, and was " unco' gracious," for I'm Scotch sometimes, and you know what William Black says—

" From Hudson's Bay to the Rio Grande,
   The Scot is ever a rover ;
In New South Wales and in Newfoundland,
   And all the wide seas over."

Well, he's a chummy rover, too, and this faithful servant of the great lady, Maud Lord, filled me up with " facts " about spiritualism.   There's always a crowd ready to do that for the press, and sometimes they get a fool like the Sydney man—who's at it now —to print it.

In the room where the seance was about to take place there were about 20 chairs.   Each window and door, except the one we entered by, was carefully covered over by thick oilcloth, so that no ray of light could enter, for the spirits do not act well in the light.   That's curious, isn't it ?   There were over 20 people in the room, each of whom had paid a dollar for admission—except the press—so it was fairly profitable.   That would make over four pounds of our money !   The medium knew a lot of the people, and set them all in order in a circle on the chairs, herself occupying a chair in the centre. She had a guitar in her hand and a small box beside her. When we were all in order, and the medium was familiar with our positions, I was asked to put out the light, which was just beside me. I did so, and the darkness was painful. We were all to hold each other's hands, so as to complete the circle. Then the medium commenced tapping our knees. I wondered what that was for, but a little fat woman at my side soon enlightened me. She gasped out, "I felt a spirit hand touch me!" and I found out that was the idea all round the circle. It was so utterly idiotic that. I couldn't believe white people could be such fools—yet they were. I let go my hold on the fat woman's hand and waited for the next tap. It came right on my hand, and I grabbed the medium's fingers ; there was no mistake about that. She didn't touch me again for some time.

In a little while she said, "I see two fair children standing beside you." As it was pitch dark nobody could tell who "you" was meant for, but a man's quaking voice said, " Beside me ?" " Yes," she replied ; and then she told the miserable sinner that the spirits were his children ; they were looking at him with yearning eyes, and evidently longed to speak to him. Then she asked him if he had two children in the spirit land, and he said, " Yes ;" and the fat woman at my side said, with a gurgle of admiration, " Isn't it wonderful !"

Next a man got a tap on the knee, and was informed that four sweet children were a-gazing at him. He remarked, apologetically, that he only had three across there ; but the medium said the fourth was " very young, it never was named ; you never knew it ; it blossomed on the other side ;" and the man adopted the spirit kid, and there was great joy over the medium's poser. It was wonderful ; but when you found out that she knew several of the sitters, it didn't sound so very wonderful after all.

One woman was informed that she had "five mothers" in the better land. There was a gasp of astonishment at that, but it was all right when the medium explained it. One was her own mother, another was her husband's mother, and, as he had been married twice, there were his two mothers-in-law. That's easy, isn't it? Some of these spiritual truths are only spiritually discerned, but they are easy enough when you understand them.

When the medium made a guess that was out of it altogether, a whisper would be heard in the black darkness, " No, not him," and somebody in the circle would whisper, " The spirits are calling you, Mrs. Lord." Then the medium would hear (?), and the guessing would begin again. At times there was an odour of flowers, as though the medium had drawn a handkerchief out of her pocket, and the little fat woman and her gang would gasp, " Oh, the heavenly odour!" " Oh, the lovely flowers !" as though heavenly visitors were bearing sweet gusts of celestial fragrance to earthly nostrils. It seemed utterly incredible that such things should fool sane people, but they certainly did there.

I never got a message from the spirit land in my life, because I never knew the name of the spook that brought the message, but I had made up my mind to know the next ghost that came along, whether I knew it or not ; so when I got a smart rap on the knee, telling me that a spirit was standing beside me, I was ready.

CHAPTER II.

The medium said "There is a spirit standing beside you ; she is calling you by name. She is saying 'Paul,' or ' Peter,' or some name that begins with P." That was all right, for that was my newspaper name on the particular paper that I was there representing. You see my pseudynom was " Peter Annet," and the

medium only knew me by that name, for it was on
my card. All the pressmen of the city knew my real
name, of course, but Mrs. Maud Lord didn't happen
to know it.

"It's Peter," I said.

"Yes, Peter Annet, I think ? "

"Yes, that's me."

Questions of grammar never trouble spooks nor
pressmen when out for the night.

"She is looking at you yearningly (all spirits
seem to yearn, or long), and her name is Ella, or
Millie, or something like that." You couldn't tell
exactly what name the medium said but I wasn't
going to be fooled any more, so I said, "Is it Ella ? "
"Yes, that's the name."

Now Ella was a bouncing Jersey girl who
boarded in the same house with me, and wasn't
within millions of miles of where some of us used to
think the spirit land is. But, so long as Ella was
looking yearningly at me I felt on solid ground, and
when the medium spoke up I knew just what to say.
There was a mournful tremor in the medium's voice
as she told me about Ella, who seemed to be my
deceased mother, or my deceased wife, or some other
defunct relative, as might happen to suit. It ought
to have been real affecting when the spook's voice—
not behind me though—said "Dear Peter," and the
medium said, "She stands looking at you with great
yearning eyes ; she reaches out her arms ; she wants
to kiss you," and I murmured softly "Let her ;" but
she didn't! Poor Ella, she came several times during
the evening, but we never got any better acquainted.
I told her all about it when I got home that night.

A little later on during the evening I had another
visit ; it was deeply interesting. There came a
ghostly whisper from out the awful darkness from
where the medium sat : "Uncle Peter ! Uncle
Peter ! " I said, "Hello !" Whereupon some little
angels whispered, "Uncle Peter, we're all here ;"
and I said I was so glad. No little children on earth

h\d ever called me "Uncle Peter." No baby voices
had ever filled my listening ears with the soft cry of
"Uncle Peter," and it seemed wonderfully sweet to
be "Uncle Peter" to the angels. It would have
been worth a dollar if I had paid the fee. When an
account of this little escapade appeared in due course
in the papers, the wicked pressmen used to bail me
up in the public streets and say, "Hello, Uncle
Peter, come and have a whisky!" There's no sense
of reverence in the average newspaper man. He is
almost past praying for.

In the middle of all the miserable spirit-voice
business and yearning and angel-whispers the medium
took up the guitar and started swinging it about,
thumming on the strings with her fingers—not play-
ing a tune, mind, but simply thumming as a heedless
child might do. I wondered what that meant, but
the little fat woman opened my eyes. She gasped
out, in her gurgling, admiring little way, clasping my
hand spasmodically, "Oh, the heavenly music! Oh,
the sweet music!" When people want to be fooled
it's fearfully easy to fool them. When the "music"
ceased the medium dropped the guitar on to the floor,
and I felt the handle of it rear my foot, so I reached
out and seized it and fixed it between my legs.
"The next time the angels want any music," sez I
to myself, sez I, "they'll come for the instrument."
When, a little later on in the evening, there was a
call to "Dear Mrs. Lord" for some more music, I
could hear the spirits feeling round the floor for the
guitar; but they couldn't find it, poor things, and
they didn't know enough to come to me for it either,
poor things.

There were three men in the circle who were
strangers to the medium, and every time she tried to
fix up a message for them she struck a snag; she was
wrong every time. They wouldn't have spiritual
kids foisted on to them, nor deceased relatives of any
kind, and things got mixed. Finally, the gas had to
be lighted and a re-arrangement made and Mrs.

Lord took good care to fix the men's faces in her mind while she was placing them afresh. After that she tried her hand on them again and got along a little better, for she knew which was which now, but they were not good subjects.

During the change I lost my little fat woman, and found myself next to a delicate, sweet-faced, hysterical, sorrow-smitten woman. She had volunteered to leave the circle when it was so crowded, as she could "come in any time;" but she was kept for a hideously cruel purpose. After the light was put out once more we had some "materializations." The medium had a box with her, and out of this she had apparently taken some gauzy material, with a dab of phosphorus on it. This she swung round her head, and as the folds of cloth opened and revealed the phosphorised part, the little fat woman and her stupid gang nearly went into fits of spiritual admiration. They actually thought they saw faces and figures and ghostly apparitions; but the fraud was so palpable, so glaring, so shallow, that I was astonished. That medium must have been a genius not to laugh right out. If men and women could be brought to believe that the trickery of Maud Lord was spiritualism, then indeed any belief is possible. Bah! we are fools!

" Surely all life is a dream, mis-begot of Olympian derision,
    And the divided, strange courses of men are but dreams
        within dreams."

When the wild excitement of this "materialization" was over, there came a tap on the knee of the trembling lady at my side, and the voice of the medium said, "I see four little spirits, dear, sweet little spirits standing beside you, and they are calling 'mamma, mamma.' The sickly woman trembled like a leaf and whispered fearfully, "I had only two."

"Yes," said the medium, "only two are your very own, the others were adopted; but they call you 'mamma' in the spirit life."

"Yes, that's right," said the sweet-faced woman. "I adopted two little orphans in place of my own ; but they died, too," and she cried like a child when she thought of her loss. Just as she seemed to be going off into hysterics there came a terrible pull and a jerking at her shawl—a light gossamer thing it was —and a voice whispering, " We want to give you mesmerism ; we want to strengthen you. you're weak ;" and the little fat woman on the far side gurgled, " Oh, how good !" Then from the dark centre of the dark circle came the whispering voice, " Mamma, mamma, don't mourn for us, we're better off," and the poor, feeble, grey-haired soul replied through her tears, " I'm so glad, my darlings ;" and there was such motherly pathos in her voice that I could have cried with her, but the desire to curse the wicked sorceress in the centre was fearfully strong. The people in that circle believed as sincerely in Mrs. Lord as other people believe in their Lord ; but it is difficult for a pressman to be always civil or always silent when he sees such things going on in the name of religion, or of what passes for it.

There was much more of miserable buffoonery, but it was of a low type. The sitters were ready to laugh at ghostly jokes or to weep over ghostly sorrows—a soft-hearted, soft-headed lot—and there was not one there that appealed to my heart, except the sickly mother who wept for her dead children.

When the gas was turned up the crowd shook hands with the medium and told the wonderful things they had seen, and Mrs. Lord must have enjoyed it greatly. She came to me and said, " Well, sir, are you satisfied?" I said, " Oh, yes, perfectly satisfied ;" but she was a woman with a level head and saw what I meant. She left. Her Scotch henchman said, " Well, Mr. Annet, what do you think of Mrs. Lord now?" " She is a very smart woman," I said. Then he took me to his private room and poured out his admiration for Mrs. Lord, till it suddenly dawned on him that I was " having him." Then—aha, sweet reader—then he would fain have flung me upon the unfeeling stones of that great and exceeding wretched city, but—he didn't.

CHAPTER III.

One day, in the town of Las Palmas, in the Canary Islands, I asked a man in Spanish the way to a house I was looking for.   He answered in Spanish, giving the required directions, but I chipped in with, " I hear by your Spanish that you're English."   He burst out laughing and said, in the broadest Milesian, " Well, man, but it's quare how you could tell that." Then I said, " By your English I hear you're Irish," whereupon he laughed consumedly, and said what any other well-balanced Irishman would have said— " Come and have a drink."

Now, that Irishman and I belonged to the same race, somehow, but there's no word in our language, to call that relationship by name.   These English, Irish, Scotch, Welsh, Australian, Canadian, American people are all one tribe.   We turn up our noses at each other in fine weather ; but in bad weather we all say D——, and stick to one another like leeches. Please let me call the crowd Englishers !   We all try to speak English, don't we ?   Well, these Englishers are the most conceited people on the face of the earth.   They have the best laws, the best language, and the best religion on earth, no matter where they live.   They take it for granted that all the world outside of their circle is lost in the midst of barbarism and idolotary.   There is a wild and savage satis-faction in knowing that the Moslems are sending missionaries to England now, and they are making many converts.

Amongst these Englishers there are an enormous number of sects, aye, and religions ; but the last one

is Spiritualism. That is a good religion, if people are
good, and nobody would throw stones at it if its disciples would behave themselves—but they don't.
They set all the laws of the universe at defiance and
make such wild statements as to make an honest
man's hair stand on end. Now, I'm an honest man—
at least as honest as I can afford to be in these times
—and I want to investigate spiritualism. I want to
know what it means. But along comes a "friend of
the cause," like the reporter who is on the job in
Sydney now, and he write such infamous rot
that I never want to meet a spiritualist again.
Such writers do more to disgust the world with
spiritualism than all its enemies could ever do. There
are thousands of men like myself who are honestly
anxious to know what this dark, mystical, ghostly
religion means. It seems to deal with new forces,
that we all our lives have tried to reckon with, and
have come to believe in—

> "That fixed arithmic of the universe
> Which meteth good for good and ill for ill,   ·
> Measure for measure unto deeds, words, thoughts,
> Watchful, aware, implacable, unmoved."

Spiritualism pretends to deal with the occult
forces of the world, such as are governed
by the living spirits of long dead people. It pro-
fesses to conjure people from the abyssmal depths
where spirits bide, and hold communion with them, but
when men like myself want to investigate the matter
we are met either by the demand at the door for " a
guinea a sitting," or else by irrelevant trickery.

Here is this Sydney reporter investigating the
phenomena of the new religion, and he relates a
fearful lot of trash about a door that was pushed to
with considerable force. What has that got to do
with spirits? There are more forces in the world than
I understand. What is electricity? Herbert Spencer
says, and it is, surely, true, " The simplest phenomena in their ultimate essence are unknowable."
What force shuts the door? What force rings the

bell ? What is force? What has this force to do
with spirits?

Then a crowd of them sat round a table with
" Maggie," the medium, and the lights were put out,
and a tambourine went on the wallaby, and the
reporter felt finger tips on the back of his hands, and
" Maggie " got a crack in the ear from—a spook!
Any spirit that would strike a woman in the dark is
not fit for decent society. It left a red mark on
" Maggie's " cheek, so it must have been a pretty
solid spook ; and if I've got to believe that, before I
can go to heaven, then I may as well look out for
an asbestos shroud at once. It is so utterly imbecile
that it is difficult to believe that Englishers
can be in the swim at all, but they are!

This reporter who is now doing the spook
business in Sydney, tells a yarn about a little black
girl spook named " Cissy," who kissed a gentleman on
the forehead and left some sticky stuff on his face. It
was found to be chocolate cream! Fancy a spook
eating chocolate cream!

"Another story is told of a spirit, known as
' Geordie,' who frequently materialises for the circle
frequented by my informant. On one occasion he
did so in a room on the private premises at the rear of
a stationer's shop in Melbourne, and, being supplied
with writing materials, wrote a letter addressed to a
resident in Sydney. He was then informed it would
be necessary to stamp the letter, and replied that he
had no money. A lady present produced sixpence,
whereupon ' Geordie ' walked into the front shop, and,
to the consternation of the assistant, who nearly
fainted at the sight of his strange customer, asked for
a two-penny stamp, which was given him and with
which he returned to the sitting-room. He was then
told he should have got fourpence change, which
' Geordie ' went back for, and having obtained it gave
it to its owner. At a seance some twelve months
afterwards the same lady being present, ' Geordie '
again materialised, and was asked by the lady if he

remembered her. 'Yes,' said he, ' I gave you your change, didn't I ?"

That is certainly the worst yarn I ever saw in a newspaper. It is such an awfully tough yarn that if I were not a total abstainer I would go and have a nip, just to enable me to refrain from swearing. If there are such mutton-headed spooks as " Geordie " kicking about the other world then hell has a new terror added to its list.

Of course, a reporter is only human, and liable to err, and is also open to sympathise with the wily Hindoo who sang—

" For who hath grieved when soft arms shut him safe,
And all life melted to a happy sigh,
And all the world was given in one soft kiss."

A reporter is sadly, softly, sweetly human, and you never can tell for certain what he will say or do; but think of this fat-head explaining the complex phenomena of materialisation. He says that:

" Materialisation, that is the visible and substantial presence of temporarily re-embodied spirits, is said to be sometimes accomplished in a bright light, either natural or artificial.

" The explanation of the method in which they then become not only visible, but tangible, is that the form or portion of the form (for sometimes it con-sists of only head and bust) is composed of particles substracted from the medium and other members of the circle—thus it is stated that a considerable loss of weight is sustained by the medium during materialisation, as tested by a weighing machine.

" It is averred that it is quite usual to weigh the spirit forms, and that the weight corresponds to the aggregate · loss of weight sustained by the members of the circle, particularly the medium ; thus, supposing the normal weight of the latter to be, say, 7st. 6lb., if weighed during materialisation she will show a loss of 2st. or over, and only turns the scale at perhaps 4st. 12lb. or 4st. 13lb., whilst the other persons present will also lose weight, but in a less degree. As to the drapery difficulty, that is met in a similar way, the stuff surrounding the spirit forms being similarly materialised from the particles of the clothing and other textile fabrics which may be in the room, and I am assured that in apartments where materialisation frequently takes place the curtains ultimately get thin and attenuated by the loss of material, a certain proportion of which is dissipated in the surrounding space, and, therefore, permanently lost to the original articles from which it was taken. The same thing may apyly to the fleshy particles of human beings laid under contribution, but we know. of course, that living bodies have a power of recuperation, and of replacing atoms thrown off the body by various natural means.

" The above is given as the explanation why the drapery, in which the materialised forms are enwrapped, is usually of the simplest character, generally being merely folded round the figure in classic fashion, although I am assured that occasionally the forms appear in modern habiliments, equal in appearance to the production of a fashionable tailor or dressmaker, and sometimes adorned with apparently valuable articles of jewellery.

"I am not aware of any of these latter having been obtained and preserved, although I am told that pieces of the drapery have been cut from the raiment, and I have been shown locks of hair cut from the heads of the spirit forms and preserved as souvenirs.

" That is explained by the supposition that they have the power of permanently materialising a limited portion of their form and drapery."

After that some respectable spiritualist ought to rise and smite this reporter hip and thigh. Perhaps he is writing sarcastically, as it were, and is only taking a rise out of the spiritualists ; but if so he ought to be kicked for making fun of them. If he is in earnest, then heaven help the press which has such a representative. Perhaps he is only making a mockery of the whole thing, and may do some good, for I think it was Horace who said—

> " Men who are more impervious as a rule,
> To slashing censure than to ridicule."

CHAPTER IV.

There was once a good Christian man whe had resolved on devoing his life to the spiritual needs of the ironworkers in one of England's dark corners. He found that the people were as ignorant of Gospel truths as the wild savages in far lands. He selected one good, ignorant soul to whom he resolved to teach the Bible story, and so he began with Adam and Eve, and related the story of Creation. No book in this wide world is more intensely interesting than the Bible, and the pity of it is that most of us are so ignorant concerning its beauties. Many of the Bible stories startled the puddler very much, especially the one about Jonah. He said, "Must I believe that?"

"Well, said the pious man, "it is part of the Bible narrative."

"Oh, well," said the iron-worker with a sigh, "go on."

Another day the teacher told him about Shadrach, Meshach, and Abednego, who were cast into the fiery furnace. Now the puddler knew a good deal about furnaces. That was his business, and so he turned angrily on the pious chap and said—"Do you mean to say as that 'ere furnace was as 'ot as mine?"

"Seven times hotter," said the teacher.

"And they wasn't burned?"

"Not the smell of fire upon their garments!

"Now, that'll do you," said the puddler. "I don't believe that yarn, nor I don't believe that fish story neither."

That iron-worker represented a large number of us. · There is no sense in doubting one story simply because you don't believe another, but we all do it, just the same. When the spiritualists tell you one yarn that is utterly unreasonable and unbelievable you doubt their statements in other directions. Here am I, a man very anxious to know the truth about spiritualism. I've got real good friends who are spiritualists, and I have no prejudices against it. I don't like the idea of a fellow getting turned out of a comfortable grave to come and thump on Sydney furniture, or things like that; but if it happened I'm open to believe it. When I die I want to go to where my loved ones are, because anywhere else would be hell, and I don't want to be locked out because I don't believe. I'll believe anything that I'm able to believe, if it's necessary to do so in order to go wilh my wife to where she's going; but I can't believe some things.

Some Sydney spook-hunters have got hold of a newspaper man, and they are going to prove to him that spiritualism is true. If they prove it to him, they prove it to a large circle, for most of us want to know the truth. It ought to be easy to prove a thing like this, because if a spirit can materialise out of the solid bodies about it, and sit on a pair of Lassetter's scales and weigh seven stone five pounds, there shouldn't be any trouble about it. If a ghost from the inane can walk about and shake hands, and buy postage stamps and forget the change, it ought to be easy to make all this manifest to a clear-eyed reporter, or even to a fat-head.

Well, here's the proof. In the last issue of the paper that is now on the job, there are two sworn affadavits, witnessed and signed by a Sydney justice, to the effect that—spirits have been visiting a circle. Not at all. John Ferguson makes affirmation on

oath that a tambourine was placed on a woman's
arm, *in the dark*, while he held her arm! The tambourine had the drum broken before this happened,
but John Ferguson swears that this was a case of the
" passage of matter through matter." Mrs Annie
Mellon swears that John is right.

Look here John and Mrs. Mellon, I'll swear to
something else. When I was a small boy I saw
Professor Anderson borrow a man's plug hat and mix
a plum pudding in it. Then he cooked it, still in the
hat, and then he cut the pudding up and threw it to
us boys, and it was real good pudding, smoking hot,
and we ate it, and then he returned the hat to its
owner, and it was as nice and clean as ever it was.
That was done *in the light*, on the stage, before
hundreds of people. Talk about putting a broken
tambourine on a woman's arm in the dark! Oh,
John, if you were to go and spend a summer afternoon at Katoomba the buzz flies would eat you up,
you are so sweet and green!

That same professor came on to the stage before
us all, in the broad glare of the stage light, and took
a cloth out of his pocket. He folded that cloth up
in a curious way, and said some awful conjuring
words over it, and then he took out of it a big globe
of water, with several gold-fish swimming about in
it! Talk about a tambourine on a woman's arm in
the dark, eh! One afternoon I was buzzing about
Yokohama, in Japan, drinking saki and winking the
other eye in the " tea houses," when I came across
some conjurors. Amongst other marvellous tricks
they brought out a long ladder, and a man put it
straight up on the ground and began to climb up it.
He balanced that ladder till he got to the top, and
then he began doing tricks on it. He was clever,
and the Japs applauded. When he was finished he
pulled up the ladder to where he stood, and set it up
again and went further up yet ; and he kept going
up into the sky till he went out of sight ; and, perhaps,
John and Mrs. Mellon will meet him in the land

where the golden melons grow. You never can tell!

But what did the tambourine on the woman's arm prove? It must have been an important piece of evidence, when they met and got two sworn declarations for publication in a newspaper! Did it prove anything about spirits? It proved, perhaps, that Mrs. Mellon is smarter than John Ferguson. It proved, perhaps, that poor John is open to be fooled; but it didn't prove one iota of what we want to know. It only proved that some modern men have no more idea of the laws of evidence than the ancients had. When Moses went before Pharaoh he was to prove by a miracle that he had been sent by God, so he cast down his rod before the Egyptian king, and, lo, it became a serpent! Aaron did the same thing! but so did the magicians of the court. Aaron's serpent swallowed up the others; but Pharaoh didn't see where the miracle came in. Then Moses smote the water, and it turned to blood; but the magicians were able to do the same thing. Then Moses brought up a crowd of frogs; and so did the native magicians. When Moses tried his hand on with filling the land with lice the local miracle-workers failed; but that may have been because they were too patriotic. Anyhow, this fact stands out clear. Many conjurers of to-day do far more wonderful things than ever the spooks do, so where's the miracle?

Some of my friends believe in spirits. So do I— good spirits; but, then, look at our ancestors, they believed in things all right enough, but we know to-day that they were wrong. There was a time in "Merrie England" when they burned witches. If a woman was old and ugly and lived alone and talked to herself, that was *prima facie* evidence against her. If she kept a black cat she was surely a witch! The good people of those far away days believed her to be in communication with the spirits of evil, and one good way to test it was very popular: She was sewn up in a sack and thrown into a horse pond. If she was a witch she floated, so they took her out and burned her. If she sank to the bottom and didn't come up again she wasn't a witch, and they could fish her out and bury her; but the results were very similar to the old woman. We don't believe in that kind of thing now, in spite of the fact that we still have ugly old women who talk to themselves and keep black cats.

We don't believe in evil spirits and broom-riding witches, but John Ferguson and Mrs. Mellon want us to believe some utterly unbelievable things. I'm like the puddler. The story of the tambourine and of the spook hitting the girl in the face makes me doubt a lot of things. If I've got to believe in such yarns before I can go where some of my friends think they are going, then I may as well make up my mind to go and join a lot of noble fellows in the stock trade, who will, surely, fetch up in the same place as myself; and there we may meet Rudyard Kipling's water-carrier, poor Gunga Din. Do you remember the story of the poor Indian who was so good to the soldiers? They knew that, as a heathen, he would go to the bad place; but there's something awfully pathetic and thoroughly English in the soldier's words—

" So I'll meet him later on
At the place where 'e is gone ;
Where it's always double drill and no canteen
'E'll be squatting on the coals
Givin' drink to poor damned souls,
An' I'll get a swig in hell from Gunga Din."

The Human Eye.

CHAPTER I.

WHEN a man walks in his sleep his eyes are shut. He can see things as well as if he were awake; he can climb up difficult places and do all kinds of dangerous tricks, yet he sees not truly! He sees what he thinks he sees. That is, he thinks he sees things, and his open eye sees them, but he is not seeing what he thinks he sees. Which complicated proposition brings us back to the startling statement that you do not see with your eyes, nor hear with your ears, or feel with your fingers. The ear contains a sensitive drum which records atmospheric vibrations, and these are conveyed to the brain and registered as impressions. You really hear with your brain ; the ear is only the instrument for conveying vibrations. So with your finger. The telegraphic nerves in the finger wire to the brain "that fire is hot," and the brain wires back "take your finger away, you fool," and you do it ! But you don't feel with your finger. Some tramps went into a lime pit one night where it was warm. They fell asleep and the fumes of the lime acted on their brains. When they were found, their legs were burned off; but they never felt the pain, because the telegraphic lines were not working. That is, you feel with your brain You see with your brains, too. The somnambulist thinks he sees lakes and rivers and mountains and all sorts of things. and his eyes are open. But he has the wrong plate in his mental camera, and he photographs what he thinks he sees. Your eye is an optical instrument, a very delicate one and a very valuable one ; but it is lightly considered until it begins to fail ; then comes the moan—

> " Oh, dying years ; oh, flying years ;
> Oh, days of dimness, nights of sorrow.
> Oh, failing sight ; oh, lessening light,
> Oh, morn forlorn and sad to-morrow."

I once heard a man say whose eyes had failed him, " I'd give both my legs to get one of my eyes back." A man's eyesight is the most precious thing he has on earth. I'd rather be deaf and dumb than blind. Yet you see people abusing their eyesight in the most shameless manner, but this comes from ignorance mostly, because if there's one subject under heaven concerning which people are more ignorant than another it is the subject of eyesight. We know less about our eyes, as a rule, than we think we know about our souls. You can see people abusing their own eyes in such a way that they ought to be punished for cruelty to animals. The eye is exceedingly delicate, a most wonderful optical instrument, requiring the deepest knowledge to deal with, yet we commonly buy our glasses from the tailor, the grocer, or the ironmonger, or else from the man on the corner, and we wonder why our eyes fail early. Now I want to have a real, serious talk with a friend of mine out in the bush, and it seems to me it ought interest a lot of people, for most of us have eyes. This friend of mine tackled me on a showground about eyes, and we had a long yarn, in spite of the show, and quite a crowd got interested in the subject, so I want now to settle down to finish my story. You've got to be personal in such a story, because—well, you've got to talk from experience. I like that old idea of John Wesley's of a class meeting, where you related your own personal experience.

The first " experience " I want to relate is that of a lady. I know her very well, so you can take my word for the facts. This lady was fairly strong and healthy, but used to get the most frightful headaches. They were put down to " billiousness " and " indigestion " and sundry causes, until one day she read some remarks I'd made on eyes, and she said, " I wonder if there's anything the matter with my eyes ?" She went to a clever oculist, and you need to be sure who you go to, for there's quacks in that business as well as in every other ! I must tell you something about that later if I get the chance. The oculist examined her eyes with some weird and wonderful ins ruments, and then said, " I don't wonder at you having headaches, but I'll cure you." Now that sounded like quackery, but he turned out a pair of nose pincers for reading that were not quite satisfactory. He wanted the lady to wear spectacles, but she refused point blank. You know why ! It's foolish, of course but, still, people are that way, especially women ! He made her nose pincers (*pince-nez*, ahem !), and she said they didn't suit ; but he said they did, because the machine that he used was correct. She kept on using the glasses and reading with them, but after a few weeks she gave it up and read without them. Then her headaches came back, and she made a discovery ! Those glasses had cured her headaches, but she never missed the aches till she gave up the glasses, and they began again. She took to the glasses mighty quick, and always wears them now. There's more trouble from bad eyes, from defective vision, than anybody has any idea of, except doctors, more especially eye doctors.

I'll tell you a strange thing. I've got bad eyes. I had an accident with one, and the results were that I expected to lose both, but by a streak of luck —and a good constitution—I pulled through. But my eyes are of different focus, and one of them is astigmatic. I'll tell you what that is by and bye. My glasses are peculiar. When I leave home I've got to carry a spare pair along for fear of accidents. I can't get a pair ready made. Well, one night, some years ago, I sat in a class-room, where the teacher wrote formulæ on the blackboard. A young fellow sat next to me who never could read them, and kept asking me about them. One night he said, " May I look through your glasses ? " " Certainly," and lo, he could see first-class. He'd had bad eyes all his life and didn't know it. Soon he had a pair of glasses of his own, but when I looked through them I couldn't see a thing ; all was blurred and mixed up. Yet he could use mine. Then it dawned upon me that eyes were delicate instruments. There are more complex troubles with eyes than you could write in a month, but I must tell you one story. A young Australian lady had something wrong with her eyes. She went to an alleged " oculist " who put something in the way of a liquid into them. She suffered frightful torment, but he said it would come out all right in the end. Then he went on his holidays and the girl had to go to another doctor. He examined her eyes and said, " My poor girl, you will never see the sun again ; that stuff that has been put into your eyes has ruined them." And the girl had no remedy. She must live out her life in blindness because a certificated quack blundered. That's what makes me so careful about whom I go to with my eyes. But we'll have more talk on the subject later.

CHAPTER II.

Not long ago I was visiting a country hospital, and saw a man lying in a bed with his head covered up. The doctor took me over to him, and when the patient heard the voice of the medico he uncovered his head, for he was not asleep. He was a young man suffering from " Sandy Blight," and the sight of his eyes was enough to make you remember " Sandy Blight " for ever more. It is one of the horrible diseases that the eye of the bushman is liable to ; one of the common diseases ; one of the diseases that is put down to the "visitation of God." If there is any one phrase more than another that annoys and worries me, and tends to make me atheistic, it is that one, "the visitation of God." My God doesn't visit people with horrible blights, or take mean revenges on the chaps out in the back blocks. I wouldn't feel so bad if people said that "Sandy Blight" was a "visitation of the devil," but even that would be a libel on Beelzebub, for as was well said in the Bigelow papers—

> "I du believe that 1 should give,
>   Wut's his'n unto Cæsar;
> Fur it's by him I move and live,
>   From him my bread an' cheese air."

It's no use stopping to argue about that now, but it's not a fair deal to blame God for what we bring on ourselves through our crime or ignorance.

This young man who lay in the bed at the country hospital was suffering from "Sandy Blight." His eyelids were red and inflamed, and swelled up so that he couldn't see. His tortures were something frightful, because the primary "blight" had led to ulceration of the cornea, and he was nearly blind, even if the swelling of his eyelids had not shut out the light. What I want to do is to try and explain in simple language what was the matter with that young fellow. Those who are not interested in eyes can skip this, for I want to talk solemnly and earnestly to the boys out back.

"Sandy Blight" is really what is known as granulation of the eye-lids, induced either by cold or by the introduction of foreign matter. It begins by a feeling of having a grain of sand on the eyelid—a sore, worriting, horrible feeling. Then, if not attended to, you begin to feel as if you had more grains of sand, and every time your eyelid moves it scrapes the bright, glassy part of the eye. Nobody knows the torture of that, except those who've had it, so it's no use trying to explain it; but those of us who have had the "Sandy Blight" can understand, and those who are liable to get it can remember. When the first germs appear you can cure it as easily as taking your dinner, if you understand what it is you have got. If you take a simple antiseptic like Boracic Acid, and put three grains to an ounce of pure water, and wash the eye with it (say a small teaspoonful of acid to a pint of water) you'll be saved. But that has got to be done early. This young fellow in the hospital had been suffering from bad eyes for two years before he reached the doctor's hands. The minute grains on the eyelid, which are really living germs, had not been washed off. They had grown, multiplied, enlarged and hardened. You couldn't wash them off now. There is no remedy for them when they reach that stage, except to burn them off with nitrate of silver. The man who uses nitrate of silver on the human eye needs to know what he is about. I'm afraid of the amateur doctor! When I was a boy a carpenter took in hand to pull a tooth for me with a pair of pincers. Tom was a good carpenter, but he was no dentist! He broke the tooth, and I had a picnic. Then we both knew that carpenters can't always draw teeth. Don't you let any amateurs fool with your eyes. When there's anything the matter with your eyes go to the best doctor you can get, or else come right on to Sydney. I never go to an oculist now, because I know what's the matter with my eyes. I go to a first-class optician, like Barraclough in Sydney, and get him to fix me up; but if there was anything organically wrong with the eyes that glasses wouldn't set right he'd send me to a doctor. But I never go to a doctor. They're good things to have about though, and a first-class doctor is a boon to any community.

This young fellow in the hospital had suffered the grains to grow and grow, and as they grew they worked the cornea of the eye, until it grew dim. just as a piece of glass would do with constant scratching. Then came ulceration of the cornea, and when he came to the hospital one eye was nearly done for, and the other was not far behind. In order to save his eyes he had to have the granulations burned, and what he suffered in that bed was enough to cleanse his soul from all the sins of a long life-time, if suffering cleanses at all, which I doubt. But he could have escaped all this torment if he had only known what it was that afflicted him early, or if he had gone to a doctor at once. But doctors don't hang their shingles on every gum tree in the bush and poor people suffer a lot in hope of it passing off without medical advice. People don't always know what to do, or they neglect to do even what they know they ought to do, and when torture and blindness comes they say it is a " visitation of God."

This " Blight " is infectious at certain stages, and in some districts it is very common. But it belongs specially to dry and dusty places, where men are galloping about after stock or where they are handling sheep a lot. We are not so liable to it in towns, where there are water-carts and paved streets. but out on the Barcoo and the Never Never, and all the dry places of the land it is horribly common. When the air is so full of dust that it is scarcely safe to drive, the eyes get filled up with uncleanness, and the germs of the " Blight " are frequently there. The scorching heat dries up the flood-waters of the eye, which are there for cleansing purposes, and the microbe gets its first chance on the soft, red tissues— the mucous membrane—of the eye, and if you don't get an antiseptic wash then, you're in for it. I'm in the hands of the optician now, getting new head-lights, so eyes are a deep and awful subject to me at present. In fact, they always are, so it seemed a good chance for me to say what I've said now, and some of you will find it worth remembering.

CHAPTER III.

Some people believe in fortune telling ; some
don't. The other day an artist said to me, "that
man cheated me out of five pounds ; but I was a fool
for trusting him ; his eyes are too close together."
As I believe in character reading, and as I also believe that " whatever a man soweth, that shall he also
reap," you may say that I believe in fortune telling,
eh ! That artist's opinion coincided with an article
of settled belief that is part of my mental stock-in-
trade. Eyes denote character, and eyes are subject
to mental and physical laws, and in a sense therefore to moral laws. Shifty eyes are bad. I
like people to look me straight in the face when
they are talking to me. You can tell a fearful lot of
things by people's eyes. But very few people have
got good eyes. I think it was the great Helmholtz
who said that if an optician sent him an optical
instrument as faulty as a human eye, he would return it and refuse to pay for it. There may be something in that, but the philosophy of it is too deep
for us just now.

People get head-aches because their eyes are not
optically correct. They work for a while and get
weary, and thinking that it is the mind that is
wrong, they get disgusted and change their work ;
but, really, it is their eyes that are wrong. If they
find that out, they go to a grocer, or an ironmonger to get a pair of spectacles, and then wonder
why things are still wrong. Eyes are delicate and
complicated things, and you should never trust anybody with the care of them except a well-trained,
able and certificated man. " Them's my sentiments."

You take my eyes. One of them is of a different
focus to the other, owing to a cold I caught sitting
on a bridge near midnight, years and years ago. I

nearly went blind over that little affair. Then, one of my eyes is "astigmatic." That is, the glassy surface isn't even. If you look into a spoon you see your face elongated. That is, because you are looking into a polished surface that is uneven. There are mirrors made to distort you in a humorous manner. One shows you long and thin, while another shows you short and broad. There are mirrors to distort you, because they are cheap, but *they* are not humorous. Your eye, if not true, distorts things, and that is "astigmatism," but that can be corrected by spectacles made by an optician who understands his business. My belief is that thousands of people suffer from their eyes, in ignorance of the cause of their troubles. If everybody who needed glasses wore them, there would be very few without them. There was a fox had his tail cut off in a trap, and he called all the foxes together and tried to persuade them that they would look better without tails than with them. I wear glasses, but I'm not arguing on the fox's basis !

The eye is a wonderful instrument and has wonderful powers of accommodation. A good eye can read the finest print, or see very small objects, and can then see the dark markings on the moon, which is 240,000 miles away. It can pick out the face of a friend across the street, and see the twinkling of a star which is 40 billion miles distant. You can't do things like that with a telescope or a microscope, or any artificial optical instrument. I had an old friend once, named Bill Jones, who carried three pairs of spectacles. One pair was for reading, one pair was for looking at things afar off, and the third pair was for ordinary use about the house. Bill was always short of one pair somehow, and then he'd make remarks, such as never were printed in a school book. He was a good man too, except when he lost his glasses ! Now, my spectacles are curious, I'm short-sighted in one eye, I'm astigmatic in one eye, and my eyes lack the power of accommodation, so that I need one pair of glasses for long sight and another pair for writing. But I couldn't possibly wear several pairs of glasses, so I have all the requirements ground in the one lens. There's about four different sights in my one pair of glasses. The upper part is to see far off, and I can see splendidly. The lower part is to work with, and my eyes are as good as a boy's, so you can understand that when I take to talking about glasses, I speak as one having authority. You can't see anything different in my glasses from the ordinary ones unless you look very close. I ought to shout for the man who made my glasses of course, for they are a triumph of optical skill. It was H. A. Barraclough, 371 George Street, Sydney, and he deserves all I can say of him. I'm proud of his work.

If a man can't read ordinary type at 8 inches or closer, then there's something the matter with his eyes As a man grows older he needs to hold the print further and further away. With my old-fashioned glasses I wrote at a distance of 18 inches. With the new improved four barrelled glasses I work at 14 inches. With the old glasses I read at 19 inches, with the new ones at 14 inches. It's wonderfully interesting to measure the distances that people read at ; but most of us never think of such things till our eyes begin to play up with us. But 'tis trouble that opens our mental eyes very often. We belong to a race that only shows its best in times of trouble, that needs for its fullest development—

> " The blood of the storm, and the blessing
> Wrapped in the rolling of vapours, and born
> Of the sun and the sea."

The world's great men have given their best thought to this matter of vision, and no subject on earth is more worthy of it. It was Professor Javal, of Paris, who invented an instrument for examining the eye. It is called the ophthalometer. I'd describe it, only that my powers of description are too feeble. Here is a picture of it :

The patient sits at one side of the big wheel and places his chin on a rest and looks at a point that he is told to look at. A strong light is thrown into his eye, and the optician marks of the defects in the eye on the machine. There is nothing left to cha ce. If the optician knows his business, that ophthalometer will tell him how the power of the eye is out of gear, and how far it is out. I was measured by this wonderful instrument, and when we had finished, I shifted the optician to the patient's place, and had a look at his optics. An eye is a wonderful thing! When I was a youngster I used to look at salmons' eyes on the river bank, and wonder, awesomely, how it was they could see with such queer shiny balls as those eyes. But when I looked through that ophthalometer, and saw the red, living fleshy tissues, and the pulsating life of the optician therein, it filled me with a more knowledgeable awe. I didn't know which to admire most—the miracle of the human eye. or the skill of Javal for inventing such a machine.

The more I see of the science of optics, the more I wonder at the way our eyes endure, considering the strain we put upon them, and the ignorance of most of us concerning them. I'd like to say a lot more on the subject, for I haven't touched many of the points that I had resolved on discussing ; but if any of you who are interested in eyes, write to me, I'll do the best I can to answer any queries that you may want to propound.

Our British Ships.

NOT many days ago a party of us went to see the great German ship, the "Friedrich der Grosse," in the dry dock at Cockatoo Island. One man in the launch [that we journeyed in was full of enthusiasm for the "Beautiful Harbour." He talked with pride and pleasure of its vastness, its depth, its beauty, and of the marvellousness of a great ship like the "Friedrich," coming so many miles from the sea to this dry dock. Said I : "You're the first New South Wales man I ever met who praised up our harbour." Then some of the passengers laughed and said : "He's a Victorian!" Then I laughed. People accuse us of boasting about our harbour ; but we don't; it's the visitors who do it. We belong to that pig-headed, colonising, *nil admirari* British race that never sees glory in its own. We Australians rarely see any good in an Australian poet, artist, musician or scholar until the folk beyond the sea have caught a glimpse of their glory. We're built that way ! But we love another deep down in our hearts, and we think our own race the best after all. Many generations of fighting ancestors have left their impress on us, and we love our own with—

> " The faith of men that ha' brothered men
> By more than easy breath ;
> And the eyes o' men ha' read wi' men
> In the open books of death."

We went up to the big dry dock on Cockatoo Island and saw the great German steamship therein. She is over 10,000 tons gross tonnage, and she *is* a big ship. Some of our people went into ecstacies over her ; but I didn't, because she was "made in Germany" It may be that on the morrow we will be at war with the Germans over the Boers, or over the new German settlement in China, or over the monkey tricks of the Emperor William, so I'm not prepared to enthuse over German ships. Perhaps that's because I'm narrow and insular and ignorant but, perhaps, it is because I love free England, and have travelled this wide world over and have seen the crushing power of military despotisms, and so my heart turns ever to the dear old Carline wife in the North Sea, of whom Kipling sings—

" Home they come from all the ports,
The living and the dead ;
The good wife's sons came home again
For her blessing on their head."

We have steamships carrying our own flag that beat the Nordeutcher Lloyds out of the field. We have ships that are bigger and better—and British. But our people are idolators and bow down and worship at the shrine of cheapness, and they sail in French and German ships to save a shilling, because the French and German Government subsidise their steamers to enable them to steal our trade. We send our wool and our freights by foreign boats to save a sovereign, and yet we sing patriotic songs and blab about our love for the old land Bah ! When war does come, we'll ask which of our people have travelled with the enemy, and which of our people have shipped their goods on the lines of the foemen, and then we'll hiss. T'were all as well to do it now ; I'm a "jingo" all right ; I confess it, and I'm not greatly ashamed of it.

One of our passengers on that day said the "Langton Grange" carried more cargo than the mighty "Friedrich der Grosse." I was surprised and pleased, for the "Grange" boats come in and out of our ports and no man makes remarks thereon. They don't go into our dry docks, either ; they don't need to ; they were built in Ould Ireland ! The nett registered tonnage of the "Langton Grange" is 3844 tons. How could she carry more cargo than the 10,000 ton German ship? This register business breaks me up. The carrying capacity of the "Langton Grange" is 9100 tons! When she goes through the Suez Canal she pays on her registered tonnage, and that is what she carries below decks, but the "Grange" has vast covered in houses on deck, on which she does not pay. Her registered tonnage is 3844 tons; her dead lifting capacity is just below 10,000 tons. She is not a passenger boat like the big German; she has lovely cabins and can carry a few passengers, but she is first and foremost a cargo boat, and we make no fuss about her. Do you know why? Because, like the "Beautiful Harbour," she belongs to us! That's why! She comes over here from London and discharges her vast cargo and then goes up North and takes in frozen meat at Bowen and Gladstone. Then she comes along the coast gathering up wool, and meat, and tallow and all sorts. When she has a few thousand tons aboard she goes off to the River Plate and fills up with hundreds of live bullocks for the London market, and nobody makes any fuss about her. She's English, that's why, and we never can see any glory in our own. We can't help it. That's the way we're built.

That "Langton Grange" can carry in her refrigerated holds 100,000 carcases of sheep, or 2200 tons of frozen beef! If you say that quick it won't sound much, but if you stop to think it's an awful lot. I don't believe I ever saw 100,000 sheep at one time in my life. When you begin to think about it you imagine that nobody else did either, don't you? That is what has abolished famine in the kingdoms of the earth. You can transport the flocks and herds of the pastoral lands to the crowded streets of the manufacturing cities, so famine has ceased to be.

When I begin to think about what ships like the "Langton Grange" carry it makes me tired. She

can carry 16,000 bales of wool besides the frozen
meat. Do any of you folks cut as much as that, eh ?
Sixteen thousand ! She carries in her bunkers 1240
tons of coal, and never a cob of it visible on deck.
The Langton Grange is a floating warehouse, a palace,
a miracle, a ship worth admiring, and she was not
" made in Germany." Ships like her come and go in
our big harbour, and we take no heed of them ; they
are the servants of the mightiest race on earth, and
we were born into royalty, and so hold cheaply the
ships and the glory of our nation ! But we rave over
foreigners. That's our little way. There's something
very good about it, too, when you come to think
of it.

   This " Langton Grange " belongs to the Houlder
Line, which has a fleet of ten ships, three of them as
big as this ·' Grange," and the tonnage of the fleet is
over sixty-six thousand tons. But the Houlder Line
makes no fuss. If you go into the Sydney office and
meet the managing director, Mr. Linley, you would
take him for an ordinary Englishman. He puts on
no side, and you'd never think he was boss of a big
world-shifting concern like this. But that's the
trouble with the race ; they don't know their own
magnificent capacity. God bless them !

   That " Langton Grange," carrying over 9000
tons, makes her way to England at the rate of 11½
knots an hour, week in and week out, voyage out,
voyage home, year after year. Her grand, modern
machinery makes me think of the cry of the " thrust
block " in McAndrew's hymn--

" ' Not unto us the praise, or man—not unto us the praise !'
Now, a'together, hear them lift their lesson—their's an'
    mine ;
' Law, Order, Duty and Restraint; Obedience, Discipline !'
Mill, forge an' try-pit taught them that when roarin' they
    rose.
An' whiles I wonder if a soul was gied them wi' the blows."

   I'd like to tell you some more about our English
ships, but my space is full ; yet I wonder at our own
people sailing in ships that were " made in Germany."

A Trip to Tasmania:

CHAPTER I.

HOW glad we were to leave Sydney wharf on a hot, sticky, Saturday morning, bound away on a 600 miles trip, to the country of the Tasmanians. Life had been so fevered of late, that it seemed as though it would be glorious to have nothing to do for a few days, nothing but to eat and drink and loaf and sleep and watch the sea. It would be grand to go without a lead pencil, or an intention, and never take a note, or write a line, but we didn't make ourselves, and good resolutions have no more effect on some people than water has on a duck's back.

We had nobody to see us off, it's best to go that way if you can, but there was a rare crowd on that steamer. We knew a lot of them, of course, for this is a very little world, yet there was a crowd to wonder at. As we steamed down past Garden Island, a tall aristocratic-looking lady stood on the starboard rail, waving her handkerchief to somebody ashore. Still she stood and still she waved, as we passed Clark Island, Darling Point and Shark Island, and then—she burst into tears and ran away down below. We saw her no more on that trip. She wasn't mad either, shews only broken-hearted. Do you know why she was leaving Sydney, or why her soul was full of the bitterness that made her independent of the judgement of strangers? I don't, but I wanted to weave a story round her, and I was sorry that I'd vowed not to write. But that woman was just like the rest of us. She had a story to her! So have we all, because we're human.

As we passed out by the Hornsby Lighthouse
a big paddle steamer bound for an excursion to the
Hawkesbury River, came out just after us, growded
with gay passengers.   The sea came rolling gently
in through the heads, and the paddle steamer began
to heave, and our passengers on the Oonah began to
—steal away to safe places.   It does me good to get
out on to the world of waters.   I love the sea, and
its everlasting, deathless motion appeals to me as
nothing else does.   Death, Time and the Sea are the
mighty servants of Eternity.   They are the scene-
shifters for life's tragedy.   They not only arrange the
pictures for the play, but they change the audience
as well.   One time the play is in Atlantis, and the
human mites work out their little lives in pride and
woe, then Death and Time and the Sea cover Atlantis,
with oblivion, and the tragedy is carried on at
Babylon, at Athens, at Rome, at London, in Australia, and Atlantis is but a vague tradition.   As we
steamed out from Sydney Heads we saw the surf rolling
gently into the Gap, where it reared and thundered
years agone with the sad relics of the mortals who
sailed on the Dunbar.   As we passed the sandhills
at Bondi, we seemed far, far from civilization, but
then we came to where the Sydney dead sleep in the
Waverley Cemetery.   It looked weird, uncanny, awful.   From our distance it looked like a rough patch
of land as rough as the skin of a thorny pineapple.
But every light-coloured speck was a tombstone, and
every tombstone stood for a human tragedy, for I
looked into some of the graves there myself and
knew some of the stories.   But now we stood afar off,
on the deck of a steamer, on the heaving, never-
resting, merciless sea, and we could watch how time
was helping Death to bring all the human ones of
Sydney to Waverley.   Life looks very different to
you when you're on the sea, gazing at a cemetery!
If we could only stop to think?   But we can't.   It's
such a hard business this making a living, that we
have no time to live.   We haven't time to lift our

eyes above the ash heaps, and it took such a lot of
worry to raise the money for this trip, that a lot of
of us never saw the Sinaitic glory of the heads, and
the cliffs and the sea, and the sky and the cemetery :

" If thou hast wanderings in the wilderness
And find not Sinai 'tis thy soul is poor ;
There towers the mountain of the voice no less
Which he who seeks shall gnd ; but he who bends
Interest on manner still and mortal ends
Sees it not, neither hears its thundered lore."

Soon after we passed Waverley and Coogee and
the home places, we passed a great big ship heading
across our track. She had every stitch of plain sail
set, and lay slogging at the waves in a helpless way,
for the wind was very, very light, and of very little
service to such a big ship. She was a big ship when
she lay at the wharf. She was a big ship measured
by other ships, but she looked such a speck of a
vessel when measured by the vastness of the sea or
even by the miles of rugged cliffs that reached along
on our starboard side, and she looked so utterly
helpless as she lay there. Soon we passed her and
she was but a speck on the horizon, a poor, pitiful
little speck that wouldn't be missed if she went right
down at once ! She wouldn't be missed by us, maybe, but what about those who had loved ones aboard
of her ? That ship is the centre of the universe to
some. She is a little world, with a very important
captain, and a swagger mate, and a bully second
mate, and a buck bo'sun, and perhaps a swell " mid-
shipman," who wears a brass band on his cap and
anchor buttons on his coat, and thinks himself a
little almighty when he's ashore. Tra-la-la. How
God in heaven must laugh at the style we little
mortals put on, eh ? You should have seen us on the
Oonah ! They had good tucker, and lots of accommodation, even for the big Christmas crowd that was
going over. When we first got out, and the big,
deep see moved itself, there was a feeling of common

brotherhood, especially among the women. But
when the wind died away altogether, and the sea grew
very calm, they began to manifest the flesh and the
devil. They put on swagger frocks and bonnets, and
they jumped each other's seats at table, and looked as
stuck up if they were the bosses of the universe. You
soon begin to find out who's who on a ship. Poor little
miserable sinners that we are, ain't we ?

There's some who were sea sick all the trip, in
spite of good weather, good tucker, and civil stewards. '
That's what makes me tired. I can't for the life of
me understand human stomachs. If we were half as
smart as we think we are, we'd freeze people, or
hypnotise people, when they went aboard ship,
if they wanted it, and take them across utterly
unconscious, then thaw them out when they arrive,
or de hypotnise them. It would be a grand thing for
people with weak stomachs. They could put on their
jewels and best clothes and things ; be chilled and
laid in a bunk, and wait there in state till the ship
was tied up at the wharf ready to go ashore. It
would save a lot of trouble. I get sea-sick if it's
rough, but my sickness takes the form of hunger. I'd
never want to be chilled or frozen, for I enjoy the
great deep and its mighty tossings ; but we are a
laggard race, in that we still allow people to suffer in
sea trips. I meant to have told you something about
Tasmania, but here's this yarn long enough, and I'm
not there yet. Never mind, the editor must be patient,
and I'll tell you about it later.

––––––––

CHAPTER II.

When I set out for Tasmania I sought far and
wide for a guide book, and got one ; but it was full of
facts. I hate facts ! Like the multiplication table,
they have their uses, of course, but I wanted to know
something of the history of the place, something of
the romance of the Island, and the guide book only

gave distances, tariffs, and things like that. Tasmania is to me a wonderful land—a land of romance and weird happenings. My first recollection of Tasmania are interwowen with the love of Abel Jansen Tasman, and as there exists a good deal of mystery about him, I'll tell you the yarn, as I remember it. About the year 1640 the Dutch Governor of Java was named Anthony Van Dieman, and he had a sweet Dutch daughter named Maria. She had a sailor lover named Tasman, and he wanted to do something grand to win her hand. The Dutch, in those days, were the great sea folk, the exploring, trading, colonising people of the earth, as our people are to-day. The Dutch-India Company was anxious to explore the southern seas, and many ships under able commanders, were sent out to find new lands. Abel Jansen Tasman left Batavia in August, 1642, in the little ship "Heemskirk," accompanied by his brother Gerritt, in the still smaller ship "Zeehan." Abel was a pious chap, as was the fashion of his day, and when a man is pious and in love, he is armed to face the world, the flesh and the devil. When he sailed away for unknown land and seas, he wrote in his log book, " May God Almighty be pleased to give his blessing to this voyage. Amen ! "

On November 24, 1642, he sighted Tasmania, at what we now call Point Hibbs, and he named the new country, not after himself, but after his best girl, "Van Dieman's Land." He sailed along the coast, and reached Storm Bay. He anchored in Fredrik Hendrik Bay, and he very nearly discovered the harbour where Hobart stands now, but a gale of wind drove him off, and he sailed on and on until he discovered New Zealand. He named an island after his darling, " Maria Island," and the record of his visit is strong on the land now, though later men altered it to bear his name, instead of his girl's. It was altered to Tasmania. I hope he got back safely to Batavia to marry his sweetheart, and lived long and died happy. He was a good Dutchman.

When I came on deck on a Monday morning and saw the basaltic, organ-pipe masses of Cape Raoul, over 250 years later, I wondered how he succeeded. That's the kind of yarn I would have liked to read, but it said nothing about it in my guide book. You would have thought that the Dutch would have come over and taken possession of Tasmania then, but they didn't. Nobody seemed to take any notice of the discovery, and Sir Joseph Banks found Tasman's diary last century and took it to England, where it is now. You see, all men were interested in the " New World " about that time, for it was only in 1620 that the " Pilgrim Fathers " landed on the—

" Bleak New England shore,"

seeking that freedom to worship God which was deniedthem in England. America was the centre of observation, and that must be the reason why Tasmania was neglected. Then, too, it was considered to be part of Australia, that great " South Land of the Holy Spirit," which nobody seemed to care to colonise, for its bleakness and barrenness and generally poverty-stricken look.

It was 1794 when Captain Hayes discovered and named the Derwent, and it was 1796 before the gallant Bass named the straits that separate Australia from Tasmania. Two years later, in Governor King's time, the little sloop Norfolk, 25 tons burden, built at Norfolk Island, was sent on an exploring expedition from Sydney, and Flinders did a grand thing—he named two mountains after Abel Jansen Tasman's little ships, the Heemskirk and the Zeehan. Did you ever hear talk of the Zeehan mine ? That recalls to me the Dutchman's love story, but it only suggests dividends to some people.

In 1800 the island was taken possession of by Governor King, for Britain, and in 1803 they shipped a lot of convicts over, who were nearly starved to death, for nobody seemed to be able to make much out of the lovely little island. We say " little " island, but it's jolly near as big as Scotland or Ireland, and those two places have made their mark in the world. Tasmania contains over 26,000,000 square miles of the finest land on the face of God's earth, and Scotland has only about 30,000,000 square miles, and there's a lot of Scotch and Irish people in Tasmania, who seemed determined that their adopted land shall be as great, as rich and as important as the old lands across the sea.

The history of Tasmania is the history of all our colonies. The first crowd that landed was a poor sample, and they did just what our people always do, they set up a rum shop and took to quarrelling amongst themselves. In 1811 Governor Macquarie crossed over from the mother colony of New South Wales—a distance of over 600 miles—and chalked out the town that was to be. He called Liverpool. street after the Minister of the day, Lord Liverpool. He called one street after himself—he was great on immortalising himself that way. Just as the average mortal writes his name on walls and shutters, and carves it on trees ; so Governor Macquarie wrote his name on towns and streets and rivers and bays. Macquarie-street is one of the great streets of Hobart now ; and Elizabeth-street, named after his wife, is the street I lived in. Then there was Argyle-street, named after his native place at home, all bearing excellent testimony to his yearning after immortality. In 1825 Tasmania was made into an independent colony, and it will yet be one of the brightest gems of the Australasian group.

Hobart has a harbour that is only second to Sydney. It is twelve miles from the entrance to the town, one of the grandest harbours imaginable, with deep water right up to the streets of the city. Seven ironclads of our squadron lay there when I was over, and they looked lost in the immensity of the habour. The land is rich in minerals, almost every valuable sotne of earth being present in the rocks, from gold to coal, from iron to diamonds. The soil is fertile, and, as a rule, well watered. The free colonists who came long ago have made much of the land, and the island has now a population of about 160,000, and as British a crowd as you can meet anywhere. They are the centre of the universe to themselves. They have their churches, their burying grounds, their Parliament, and their civil servants; and I'm proud of them. They are of the same old stock as has colonised the earth; they are as narrow, conservative and slow as any of us; but they have a debt of over eight millions sterling, and they make as much fuss over their elections as the folks at home do; but I must tell you some more about them in my next.

CHAPTER III.

I was once staying at Las Palmas, in the Canary Islands, and wanted to go over to the next island, Tenneriffe. The hotel-keeper warned me solemnly against it, as he said they had the yellow fever over there—a statement which was very heartily endorsed by many natives. Nevertheless I went and on arriving at Santa Cruz the people there said they had never had yellow fever at all; it was at Las Palmas they had it. That kind of rivalry seems to exist amongst Australians as well as Spaniards, and if you listen to the stories of Victorians against New South Wales, or *vice versa*, you will realise that federation is not such a simple thing as it looks. On arriving in Hobart I was delighted with everything I saw except the roads. It was said to be a " Cyclists' Paradise." All I can say is that I'd like to see a cyclists' purgatory. The man who invented that phrase was a liar, and the truth was not in him. I saw more cycles break down in one week in Tasmania than I ever saw in my life before, for what with steep hills and blue metal the roads are abominable.

But the climate is delightful, and the scenery beats the world. I wanted to go on to Launceston, distance by rail 133 miles. Nobody said a word against it. One man said it was well-worth seeing, but there was not as much to see as about Hobart. Remembering Las Palmas we went, and behold, it was true. It is a real live go-ahead town of about 23,000 inhabitants—including the suburbs—and it is a revelation to visit the place. We were informed that when the Melbourne boat arrived the visitors just stayed one night in Launceston, then went on to Hobart, as that was the picturesque part of the Island. Never a hard word did I hear from the north end of the island about the south end, and my respect for the Tasmanians rose considerably.

I had been told that the Tasmanians were a sleepy, lazy, conservative people. That's another lie. Here was Launceston, founded this century, with fine buildings, good roads, splendid houses, miles of streets, and the electric light. They have harnessed the river Esk, where it breaks through a dolomitic gorge, and have made it provide the town with illumination, and they are now arranging to make the river run their printing presses and machinery as well. Talk about being sleepy. Why I've seen towns of 75,000 inhabitants in the United States that were not nearly so progressive or enlightened. The Tasmanians are not so feverish in their lives as we are ; they have more sense, they live easily and comfortably, and live long. Their exports last year amounted to £1,305,160, and for a population of 160,000, there's nothing sleepy about that.

The disappointment about Tasmania to me was its exceeding orthodoxy. When a stranger lands at the railway station at Launceston, it looks as if he had struck an old English town. There's the cabman who fleeces you—the porter who touches his hat, the giggly girl who has come to meet her "fellah," and

the hopeless, idle, good-for-nothing, who is the pro
duct of city civilization everywhere. In the town
on a Saturday night you have the same bright shop
windows, the drifting crowds, the fried-fish shop, the
gift-tea shop, and the draper who is making "enormous sacrifices." The people speak as their kinsfolk
speak beyond the sea ; they dress as all their race
dresses in the little islands of the sea whence we came
out to found this " New Britannia in a southern sea."
But the busy streets were all filled with the soft electric light, and the people seemed to be parading in the
full of a bright moon. Some people say that Tasmania
is a good country for a man to die in, but I think it's
a grand country to live in. If Launceston had been
a mining town you could have understood its rapid
development, but it stands 40 miles from the sea, up
the great River Tamar, where there is only a depth
of about ten feet at low water, and the town has been
made by the genius and enterprise of our own
colonising people.

Hobart itself, the southern capital, where Parliament sits, and where Government House stands, is
a perfect marvel of a place. They have good
wharves, where the biggest ships can lie, good streets,
fine buildings, and the electric tram. The population
of the town and suburbs is about 36,000, and I'll
back it against any town in the world for its size.
It is surrounded by hills, or

> "Mountains, that like giants stand
> To sentinel enchanted land."

Mount Wellington stands just behind the town,
forming a magnificent back ground. and the scenery
all round is simply delightful, while there are wonderful places to visit within easy distance. It is
an ideal place for a holiday, and the harbour
assures it for ever as a place of resort for the ships
of the world.

They have a public library that represents the
somnolency of the place, for it has no catalogue,

which makes it just a little superior to a library
which has an incomplete and misleading catalogue;
but this Hobart library is only awaiting a live
librarian. The museum is a gem. It is not very
large, but it possesses one of the most delightful
rooms that I ever came across. It is the "Tasmanian Room." Here are collected all the produc-
tions of the Island, and nothing else. You see almost at a glance what Tasmania can produce from
coal to gold, from snails to sharks, from aboriginals'
skulls to the Tasmanian devil. If any man will walk
through that room with his eyes open he will see that
there is a mighty future before Tasmania. The
samples of coal alone are suggestive, but the curator,
to leave no doubt in any mortal mind, has cards
printed to tell you what is being done in the colony
in the way of coal-mining. Last year they mined
over 33,000 tons of coal. Last year the output of
gold was £212,329, and that of silver £175,000,
and of tin £145,000. Then some people have the
cheek to say that Tasmania is sleepy, stupid, and conservative. That room was the sight of the island,
because it grouped all the facts of island history in a
picturesque manner, and showed the stranger what
the country was capable of. Geologically, Tasmania
is the epitome of Australia. It contains almost every
known rock and stratum known to geologists, and
its vast resources are being developed every day.
This room in the museum shows you all the known
products of the place, and the curator—who, by the
way, came from the Sydney Museum, Mr. Morton
—deserves the thanks of all who love Tasmania for
his wise and patient labour.

I would like to add that the Tasmanians I met
were nice people, kind, obliging and helpful. They
have a good country, they live easily, they grumble
a lot, and they are cursed with a Parliament, but they
are just as pleasant a lot as you'd want to meet anywhere. When we do come to federate, this little
Tasmania will be a power in the ranks of the federated

colonies, for she is rich and she is wise, and she is in no hurry. She has mighly lakes, hidden in the heart of the great hills, that will supply her with endless power ; she has fertile valleys that produce the finest fruit in the world, and millions of acres of uncleared land awaiting the population that has yet to come.

> " Complete she lies
> Within the unbroken circle of the skies,
> And round her indivisable the sea
> Breaks on her single shore."

CHAPTER IV.

In the year 1817 Lieutenant Governor Davey laid the foundation stone of St. David's Church in Hobart. It was a great day, for the Governor was a strange man. He served out half a pint of spirits to all the convicts and soldiers, and the little town went fairly on the razzle-dazzle. Davey used to go on the spree with the " boys," and some of the stories told about him would almost make your hair stand on end. Still the colony progressed under his rule, and it may be that neither Davey nor the devil are as black as they are painted. Remembering the incidents of that olden time I gladly accepted an invitation to go to church at St. David's Cathedral on a Sunday morning, just to see what progress had been made in St. David's since Davey's day.

The cathedral is new and bright, and befitting a swagger little town. The tall, fluted stone columns were suggestive of ancient sacredotal edifices, and the stained glass windows were as medieval and orthodox as the heart of a worthipper could desire   The chancel was paved with black and white marble like a Masonic Hall, and the brass crosses and white flowers were worthy of a well-dressed church parade. The large male choir was dressed in purple robes and white surplices, and the parson wore a white stole. When we had got seated and smelled our hats the services and my trouble began. There was a very young man, with a very feeble monotonous voice, began to chant the glorious words of the service. You couldn't tell a word he said, and he had such a sanctified snivel and such a holy drawl that it worried me out of worship altogether.

Once upon a time I made a passage from New-castle-on-Tyne to Constantinople, and the skipper was an Episcopalian. I was the only passenger, and on Sunday we used to have a little service down in the saloon. He read the lessons, and I read a sermon of F. W. Robertson's, and I enjoyed the whole thing, for the words of the Church of England service are very lovely, and fit the needs of poor humanity. They appeal to me strongly, and if I don't go to a swell church I enjoy them, but as soon a sing-song curate begins to mock God with mellifluous measure, I'm done. There's no sense in it, and I begin to grow irreligious. I begin to look round and wonder, and think about all kinds of things. When late comers arrive and put down their sunshades, their hats and sticks, and kneel in their pews to look through their fingers, I wonder what they are thinking about and what they are saying, or if they are thinking or saying anything, and I wonder if the service does them any good. Then, as we rise up and sit down, and go through the show that has lost its power to charm one, I begin to think about the thousands, even in little Hobart, who never go to church. You hear people ask, " Why the masses are not at church ?" But as I sat in St. David's I found the answer. The total effect of the service on me was that I wished I had brought my swell suit and my silk hat and my gloves, so that I could have come to church and looked like a toff. If that is the effect it had on me, can't you understand the effect it would have on the rest of the crowd if they had come ? There was a curate once said to a kid, " John, what is your father ?" "Please, sir," said John, "he's a Christian ; but he's not workin' now." That's it. Those are the sort of things I think about when I go to church and can't understand what is said. If they say the prayers in Latin, or in a foreign tongue, I can give them credit for lots of things, but when they snivel them in my own tongue and I can't understand them, then I get out of sorts and say things.

I once went to a little corrugated iron church in the market place of Tangier, when the sounds of the Arabs in the market place mixed with the words of the service ; where the wailing of Arab music mingled with the organ tones of the church. There sat beside me the wreck of a noble Englishman—a Church of England clergyman—who had sought the shores of Northern Africa in the last stages of consumption. As the words of the prayer-book came solemnly forth from his friend in the reading desk, they seemed to mean so much to him and to me, and and the whole glory of the grand passages broke over me. A few days later the sick one breathed his last, and we carried him to the little grave-yard belonging to our people, where we laid him beneath the palms, amid the glowing African vegetation, and once more the solemn words of the church rang out. Ah, me ! the service means a lot, so long as a school-ruined, college-cursed orthodox nincompoop does not murder it. I think I'd be religious if I didn't go to church, for I can't stand orthodoxy, because I believe that—

> "Slowly the Bible of the race is writ,
> Cut not on paper leaves, nor leaves of stone ;
> Each age, each kindred adds a verse to it
> Texts of despair, or hope of joy or moan :
> While swings the sea, while mist the mountain shroud
> While thunders surges burst on cliffs of cloud,
> Still at the prophet's feet the nations sit."

I sat in Davey's great church, and listened to the kids in purple frocks intone the responses. I heard the good young man, with no redeeming vices, sanctifying his vowels in a perfect manner, that had neither sense nor soul in it, and my mind went back to Davey and his convict gang, to the little town of 80 years ago, and my soul was filled with awe. When the choir arose I expected to hear the clink of the felon's chains, and when the parson crossed the chancel I wondered if he were a free man or a lag ; then I looked at the congregation, and the mists faded away. We were all free here, free from the felon's chains, but bound by the stupid old customs of dead and gone ages and times. Oh, the cant and humbug and stupid hypocricy of the age! If I were a parson, preaching the everlasting Gospel of God in a place like St. David's Cathedral, with all its short, weird, awful history, I'd shake the dry bones of the place, or I'd go and drown myself. We have a canting, swelling hide-bound gang of parsons in our churches that make me tired and sick. They have beautiful buildings, lovely music exquisite surroundings, and a grand history, and yet they snivel and whine and are impotent for good. We who love good dare not speak out, lest people should think that we are infidels and against God, so we sit silent, and watch the church go to the devil, and then we have the infernal impertinence to wonder " why the masses are not at church !" " Them asses " have sense.

CHAPTER V.

You remember that story about the bullock puncher on the Bourke-road? A Salvation Army woman said to him, " If you swear at those bullocks you'll never get to heaven." Said he, " I know that, ma'm, but if I don't swear at'em I'll never get to Bourke. Well, lots of people have that idea about bullocks, but it's wrong. I saw men working bullocks in the bush in Tasmania, and they never swore at 'em, and yet the bullocks worked splendidly. It was a queer place, too. We took the coach from Hobart

and drove about 40 miles, through the lovliest scenery
on earth, down the valley of the Huon, where the
apples come from. It's a perfect paradise of a place,
where great hills, fern clad gullies, splendid orchards,
and a lovely river. We drove through little towns
and over bridges, up hills and down hills, till we came
to Geevestown. All the books say :—This township
owes its name and origin to Mr. William. Geeves, a
native of Fowlmere, Cambridgeshire, who, with his
three sons, started in January, 1850, to carve a home
out of the primeval forest, and six months later had
established a little colony of 37 souls."

That sentence is copied into all the books, and
the inventor of it must feel proud. I think it was
the phrase, " primeval forest," that made it popular.
But the " township" amused me, because it's so
little, so scattered, and so savagely teetotal. There
are about 500 inhabitants in the place and not a
public-house or an hotel. Nobody is very rich and
nobody is very poor. The men with wives and
families work for 20s. a week, and a lot of them drop
their H's. It's horribly English only for the lack of
beer. Geeve's sawmill is the great place of the
" township," and the men work there for about 4s. 6d.
a day, and are content. But somehow that kind of
thing doesn't appeal to me, except in the way of
being glad that there is such a grand " Hinterland "
for raising sturdy, patient workers for the more
fevered life of the cities. I don't think I admire
patient, contented people, because there's seems so
much to do in the world; and I prefer unsatisfied
people, ambitious people, restless people, but not dis-
satisfied people. I'm wrong, of course, but that's
why I could never write an orthodox guide-book.

We got accommodation at " Hillcrest," a fine
boarding-house, kept by one of the Geeve's, and it
was pleasant to stand on the balcony of the house
and look around at the village, with the sawmill in
the centre, and the hills rising on every side about
the gurgling, bubbling little Kermandie River.

It was named after Captain Huon Kermandec, a French explorer, but has gotten altered a bit to suit our Saxon tongue. On all sides rose the gentle hills, and beyond them lay the rugged peaks of the Hartz Mountains. The vegetation seemed much the same as our own, dark and sad, except where the fire-king had kissed the bush and made it blush a startling red. The gaunt, white dead gum trees stood out in bold relief, where the axe of the settler had ringed the giants for destruction. It was a lovely, peaceful place.

We went off one morning with a lunch and a billy to ride on the tramway to where the loggers were at work, and that was a trip worth going to Tasmania for. The tramway was a wooden line of rails laid for over four miles through the bush to where the great forest of trees raised their crowns skyward, and there was not an iron nail in all the length. It cost over £200 a mile to build, and these contented teetotallers were the engineers and the navvies. It was a wonderful line, truly, and I never saw such a thick scrub in my life. My idea of scrub was that of thickly-growing small trees and dense undergrowth, that cattle could tear through when they got frightened and bolted, but this was so thick that a pig couldn't get through, nor a rabbit, hardly a snake. And the trees! They were the mightiest trees I ever saw in Australia, standing two and three hundred feet in height—blue gum, swamp gum, white gum, stringy bark, peppermint and sassafras.

We rode on trollies about two feet high, with low, broad, iron wheels, drawn by three horses. It was a long ride, but it was grand and awe-inspiring. When we stopped at last, beside a stationary engine, we were in the "forest primeval" indeed, and no human heart could—

> " Resist the sacred influences
> Which from the stilly twilight of the place,
> And from the gray old trunks that high in heaven
> Mingled their glossy boughs and from the sound
> Of the invisible breath that swayed at once
> All their green tops."

Beside the tram line there stood an engine and
boiler. On a great drum was a coil of wire rope,
500 yards long. Two patient, well conditioned
bullocks, Nelson and Leopard, stood near by. At the
word of command—not a swear word—they backed
up to the end of the wire rope and drew it from the
drum, and hauled it away up a long alley, cut by the
loggers in the deep, dense scrub, among the giant
trees. When the bullocks had reached a fallen tree,
the wire rope was chained to the great log, a big
steel shoe was put beneath the end, the signal was
given, the engine began to wind up, and the log, one
hundred feet long. without a branch, a knot, or a
fault, began to walk through the solemn shades. It
was a wonderful business, and the way those oxen
seemed to understand it all, without a single swear
word, was a revelation.

The wives and children of the loggers had come
up on a picnic, and the rosy, sturdy children
scampered through the shaded pathways, making the
dark woods ring with their noisy glee. They stood
by us as we watched their fathers fell a tall and
stately gum tree, whose head seemed to reach the
clouds. One man cut a big gash on one side of the tree,
the side towards which it was to fall. Two others,
with a saw, cut deep into the other side, and then the
fathers cried, "Look out, children!" and the mighty
tree bowed its stately crest, and came crashing to the
earth with a thunderous sound that was apalling. It
carried great boughs, small trees and all opposition to
the earth with it, and lay a fit object for the gleaming
axes of the strong-armed woodcutters. Perhaps I am
romantic, or poetic, or something of that kind, for the
fall of a mighty tree appeals to me with keen force.
How long had it taken that sky-reaching king of the
woods to grow? Ah, who could tell? No man could
say, but here was the growth of centuries cut down in a
few minutes, and only a small part of the great trunk
was used for the sawmill. What waste! But is it
waste? From the dead logs of past ages spring new

trees, new flowers, new life in every form.   There is no death, only change, for—

> " Life mocks the idle hate
> Of his arch-enemy Death—yea, seats himself
> Upon the tyrant's throne —the sepulchre,
> And of the triumphs of his ghastly foe
> Makes his own nourishment. For he came forth
> From thine own bosom, and shall have no end."

We shared in the destructive spirit of the hour, and my chum and I each swung an axe and cut down a tree—young ones truly, but the growth was so thick that it seemed no sin ; then we saw the logs on to the trollies and start on their path towards the mill, and we wondered that timber should be so cheap, when the labour of getting it was so hard. Then we wandered away and away down the tram-line and through the sweet-smelling bush to " Hill-crest," and rest and musings sweet.   Then on the morrow we sailed away on the steamer   Huon, down the broad river,   past fruitful orchards, pleasant dwellings, and miles and miles of wild scrub, to the channel of D'Entrecasteaux. We wondered why the brave Frenchmen should have explored these waters and surveyed them and charted them, and then left the English to seize on such a fertile place.   Ah, these Britishers are a wonderful grasping race. We steamed 45 miles back to Hobart to where the Squadron lay at anchor under the shadow of Mount Wellington, and as we saw the dear old flag floating at the stern of the strong warships we thought of Kipling—

" What is the flag of England ? Ye have but my sun to dare,
Ye have but my sands to travel ; go forth, for it is there."

The Secret of England's Littleness.

THE "secret of England's greatness" is a much-discussed subject. Some say it is the Bible; Kingsley said it was the east wind, which killed off the weaklings; and somebody else says it is the little streak of silver sea which makes English insularity. Most of us believe that there is a "secret" in England's greatness, but very few of us ever examine the grounds of our belief. Perhaps it's as well, too, because if we did a lot of our beliefs would break up; and that recalls the words of John Taylor. He said, "To believe without examination is no belief in reality, but merely an assent that such and such things are believed by others (Mr. Proofreader, if you don't spell "believed" correctly there will be a funeral in our office), and is, in fact, only believing that we believe." You can sit down and figure on that statement, gossips, for there's a chunk of solid truth in it. We don't believe nearly as much as we believe we believe. Now, I don't know the "secret of England's greatness," but I have very strong views in regard to the "secret" of England's littleness. There's a fearful littleness about our race, and I believe it arises from our love of cheapness!

The other day a wise and good man said, "We'll get that job done as soon as we get the tenders in." I said, "Tenders? tenders for a little job like that?" because it was only a matter of a few shillings, at most two or three pounds. He apologised for calling for tenders on the ground that there was a committee, and everything had to be done in the orthodox way. That's it; we want everything at the very cheapest rate, and we allow no man to take a pride in good, honest work, if we can help it. We must get all we can for a shilling, because we know that other men will get all they can out of us for as little as may be, so we put a premium on shoddy and dishonesty and scampishness, and the cheap man is our man. The horror of this statement lies in the fact that nobody ever seems to see it. The bargain-hunter is a good citizen, a good Christian, a good wife, a good husband, a good parent. The moment you say a " bargain-hunter " you think, naturally, of a woman who frequents " sales," who stands outside of a shop waiting for the doors to open, while she gets a chance at the " enormous sacrifices " that are being offered. The woman who does that sort of a thing is a foe to civilisation. She is a friend to the sweater and ally of the devil. But she only does it poor soul, because her husband is also a bargain-hunter, only we call him a " shrewd man of busi-ness." That's all the difference.

Some shrewd business men want the country to go in solidly for " protection " and to keep out the cheap and nasty foreigner ; but the " shrewd business man " keeps on the look out for bargains, and his wife still haunts the " fairs " and the " sales " and the " clearing out " shops, and the " below cost " places. We can see, all of us, in our sane moments —and most of us are sane occasionally—that cheap-ness is the curse of the land, but it's the other fellow's desire for a bargain that hurts, not our own. Oh, no ! We're not bargain-hunters. Why are some of so very sick and some so very poor ? Because we can make bargains and the other can't ; because one is strong and the other weak ; because men and women are born with different temperaments. But we'd all like to abolish poverty and crime and misery, but we never will so long as we crave for cheapness. London is the wealthiest city in the world, and the poorest. There is more luxury and poverty in London than in any city on earth. We, in

our Australian cities, are going exactly in the foot-
steps of the old city beyond the sea. We are
yearning for bargains and for cheapness, and
we are striving to live on the blood and sweat of
the class beneath us. We can't help it, of course,
because we were born into a rotten system, and we are
to-day what thousands of generations of blind fools
have made us. When I am taken into a " sale shop "
and see hundreds of stupid women buying rubbish
they can never use, simply because it's "cheap," it
makes me want to get up and curse their folly, or else
sit down and weep. Fools, we are all fools ! Bah !
It makes me look forward and sing—

> Kyrie eleyson !
> Christie eleyson !

when I think that an end will surely come to
the awful love of cheapness, to the bargain-hunting
curse of the earth, even if come only when —

> " There shall come a mightier blast—
> There shall be a darker day ;
> And the stars from heaven down-cast,
> Like red leaves be swept away."

Did'st ever read, Ruskin, gossips ? It seems to
me, though it's many years since John Ruskin and I
grew friends, that he objected to shams and bargains,
and the horrible love of cheapness that curses the
earth. It breeds ghastly diseases. This love of
bargains saps the moral fibre, and you'll see that
people who love bargains are afflicted with other
complaints. They aspire to be what they are not. They
will keep a lovely drawing-room for their guests, and
live in squalor in the kitchen. I know people who are so
horribly poor that they can't get a square meal for
themselves ; who haven't got decent clothes for daily
wear, yet they go into "sassiety." They go to
"functions"; they walk to parties, because they're
too poor to hire a cab. They act the grand folks,
and they talk about their relations and the aristo-
crats they pretend to know, then they tramp home
to starve, to moan, and to live false, shallow miserable

lives. That is part of the false doctrine that curses the world. Those people who want to pass for somebodies when they are nobodies, are ever on the lookout for bargains, for something they can buy for a shilling that looks as if it were worth twenty shillings. They are the curse of the earth. They set the craze for cheapness, and other fools imitate them. Some of the male bargain-hunters send their goods to England by highly-subsidised French or German steamers, and leave British ships to go home half empty. Some men go home as passengers in the foreign steamers that will one day be preying on our commerce, because—they love a bargain. But these are only the pustular signs of a deep economic disease. There's a man I know lives in a stucco villa, and has two plaster lions guarding the front door. That man can't pay his tailor nor his butcher, but he walks out proudly every morning with his nose in the air, looking as much like a "blooming toff" as he knows how. But all his neighbours see through him; they know his scheming misery and his dirty pride, and they laugh in their sleeves at him. Ah, gossips, we know one another, don't we? Our eyes are keen and our senses are acute, and we can see the tinsel nature of what the bargain hunter wants to pass off as gold. When we dare to be honest, even to ourselves, when we dare to seem what we really are, then will the world be better. Then will life be easier to all, and then will England be great indeed!